"Do You Really Know Me, Katie?"

"Do you really want to know me?" His voice was low and I thought it sounded almost menacing. I couldn't answer him. I didn't know what answer he wanted. I didn't know what answer I wanted to give.

This was Brick with the mask off, the genteel disguise peeled away. This was the Brick I had known for so many months in so many dreams.

When I still didn't reply, he threw the car in gear and roared out of the parking lot. I swallowed hard and huddled against the seat. I thought I knew what he was asking. If it was his real self that I wanted him to show me, if it was Brick I wanted, then that's what I'd get. And the warning in his voice reminded me of all the things Brick was, the smoldering, brooding passions that could not always be suppressed, the dark, unpredictable moods, the danger. . . .

Books by Ellen Conford

You
Never Can
Tell

Ellen Conford

AN ARCHWAY PAPERBACK
Published by POCKET BOOKS • NEW YORK

This novel is a work of fiction. Names, characters, places and incidents are either the product of the author's imagination or are used fictitiously. Any resemblance to actual events or locales or persons, living or dead, is entirely coincidental.

An Archway Paperback published by
POCKET BOOKS, a division of Simon & Schuster, Inc.
1230 Avenue of the Americas, New York, N.Y. 10020

Published by arrangement with Little, Brown and Company, Inc.
Library of Congress Catalog Card Number: 84-12202

ISBN: 0-671-54283-4

First Archway Paperback printing November, 1985

10 9 8 7 6 5 4 3 2

AN ARCHWAY PAPERBACK and colophon are
registered trademarks of Simon & Schuster, Inc.

Printed in the U.S.A.

IL 7+

One

THE FIRST TIME I watched *Lonely Days, Restless Nights,* was at my friend Amy's house. I must have been the only person in North High School who had never seen the show, but I didn't feel I was missing anything. After all, it was just a dumb soap.

"But it's not dumb, Katie. It's like *real life.*"

Well, it was Amy's house and she didn't want to miss even one episode, so I gave in graciously.

"Oh, all right, so we'll watch the stupid show."

"I'll tell you a little bit of the story so you know what's going on. That way you'll really appreciate it," Amy said.

"I don't want to appreciate it," I grumbled. "I don't want to know what's going on."

"Brick is trying to seduce Allison," Amy said, ignoring my graciousness. "He's a really bad person. He puts on this big, compassionate act, but he's a total phoney and he doesn't care about anyone but himself, so while Brooke is in the hospital with amnesia—"

1

"Brooke?" I said. "Brick and Brooke?"

"I'll explain about Brooke later. Anyway, Brick is the reason Brooke has amnesia, because of all the terrible things he did to her, so while she's lying there in the hospital, Brick is coming on to Allison, because she's got so much money and social status and Brooke doesn't. And Allison is beginning to fall for him, because she needs someone, especially during the murder trial."

"Murder trial?" I felt a mild stirring of interest. Not in the murder, but in the trial. I plan to be a lawyer, and I really like trial scenes.

"Yeah, Allison's mother is on trial for murdering Biff Richards, Allison's real father. So Allison is feeling sort of lost and vulnerable—you know, a perfect victim for Brick. The judge keeps calling recesses all the time. That's when the really interesting stuff happens."

"This certainly does sound like real life," I said sarcastically. "Amy, I don't really care—"

"See, Brick has this need for revenge on the whole town because he has a neurotic obsession about being poor and socially unacceptable, so he's not just a rat, but probably a little deranged, too."

Who could blame him? I was beginning to feel a little deranged myself.

"Of course, you don't know for sure that he's crazy," Amy went on; "all you know is that women are helpless in his spell and he has no conscience. I mean, he uses them and throws them away like paper towels, and even though he's blackmailing Bill Rivers—"

"*Bill?* Brick and Brooke and Biff and Bill? Why does everyone on this show begin with a B?"

Amy looked thoughtful. "There's Allison," she reminded me. "And Nicole—but you don't know about her yet. Nicole was—"

"Amy, I'm getting a terrible headache."

"You want some aspirin?"

At three-thirty Amy turned on the television.

At three-thirty-three Brick Preston appeared on the screen.

By three-thirty-eight I was madly, hopelessly, incurably in love.

I didn't even try to understand what was happening on the show, or who everyone was. I just sat there, for the next fifty-two minutes, slack-jawed and glassy-eyed every time Brick Preston had a scene. During all the other scenes, I waited for him to reappear. I didn't even pay attention to the murder trial; just the recesses.

It wasn't hard to believe that women were helpless in Brick Preston's spell. He was darkly handsome, with a hint of danger in his eyes. He wore a black T-shirt under a black leather jacket. Even from seeing only one episode of *Lonely Days, Restless Nights,* I could tell that Brick was an unprincipled, immoral, two-timing rat. I could also understand how his sinister attraction made strong women falter and weak ones crumble.

Compared to Brick, everyone on the show was bland.

Compared to Brick, everyone in the *world* was bland.

Since I am not the type to fall madly, hopelessly, incurably in love at the turn of a dial, I had no experience with the reactions I had watching Brick Preston. Even if those weren't actual heart palpitations, my heartbeat was definitely fluttery and uneven.

3

And I think my face was flushed; it certainly felt hot. My mouth was dry—probably because my jaw had been sagging stupidly open for an hour and I think I'd been inhaling more frequently than was normal. My palms, nonsweaty since I was fourteen, had become extremely moist.

Amy sighed and turned off the TV. "Isn't he gorgeous?"

"Not bad," I said. I think my voice cracked a little.

The next afternoon I ran home and waited for *Lonely Days, Restless Nights* to come on. Just an experiment, I told myself, as I paced impatiently back and forth in front of the television. Just an experiment to determine if my reaction yesterday had simply been a freak relapse into puberty; a little glandular glitch that crops up, unexpectedly, like a small tornado, to interrupt an otherwise sunny adolescence.

I looked at the clock on my parents' night table. Several times. Fortunately, my parents work at home most of the time, so if my brother, Dylan, got restless, he might bother them instead of me when he got in from school. When Attila, the Littlest Hun, gets restless, he tends to explore new frontiers in havoc-wreaking. I didn't think I could deal with any more havoc than my giddy glands were already wreaking.

Finally, three-thirty. Of course, I'd turned on the set at three-twenty-four, just in case the clock was slow or something. I'm not an overly cautious person, but I don't believe in taking unnecessary chances.

And it happened again.

Erratic heartbeat, dry mouth, wet palms.

I couldn't believe it. "This is a stupid show!" I yelled at the set. It was. It was totally unbelievable. The acting

4

was awful. The only bar the judge could ever have been admitted to was the Dew Drop Inn. Everyone was made of polyester and plastic, and no one wore their own hair.

"Except *him*." I sighed deeply.

Brick seemed to be the only real person on the show. He was not plastic or polyester and his hair was his own. Not artfully arranged and styled, but frequently mussed up by the tapering, glittery-tipped fingers of sophisticated women with an irresistible urge to muss.

What you have here, I told myself firmly, is a silly teenage crush. It will pass. It just has to run its course, like a bad fever. Eventually it will burn itself out.

This is what I told myself. This is what I told myself almost every day for the next three months, as I watched Brick Preston throw women away like paper towels. And what I told myself every night, when I fell asleep—or didn't—picturing myself in Brick's arms.

And maybe that's exactly what would have happened. I would have recovered, the fever would have burned out, I would have gone back to my nice, normal relationship with my boyfriend, Rob, and forgotten this harmless brush with fantasy.

It might have happened that way.

If Brick Preston hadn't decided to enroll in North High School.

Two

"HE'S COMING *HERE?*" Amy cried. *"Here?"*

I sank down on my bed and gazed groggily at the ceiling.

"Look at Kate," Stephanie said. "I think she's fainted." She sounded more amused than concerned. But that's Stephanie's way. She considers herself a sophisticate, and bored amusement is her style. Amy, on the other hand, is like an orange juice commercial. All open and sunny and energetic. She couldn't keep her feelings hidden if her life depended on it.

"I have not fainted," I said weakly. "I'm just resting. I'm completely alert."

Completely *in*ert was more like it. Except for the heart attack I thought I might be having. It was probably nothing serious.

"But why?" Amy demanded. "Why here? How do you know?"

"I was helping Dr. Rankin yesterday and he told me."

Dr. Rankin is a guidance counselor. Stephanie was

compiling all sorts of statistics from confidential school records for a study he was doing. Exactly what he was studying was a secret. Stephanie said he didn't want anyone to beat him to the publishers and she was sworn to keep everything the computer told her a secret also.

"By the way, I know all our I.Q.'s if you're interested in that sort of thing. Rob's too," she added. So much for confidentiality.

Amy nearly screamed. "Who cares about I.Q.'s at a time like this? *When is he coming?* And why *here?*"

"Tomorrow," Stephanie said. "Because they bought a house here."

"Tomorrow?" Amy sagged to the floor and stayed there.

"Tomorrow," I echoed. *"Tomorrow."*

"Why do I suddenly get the feeling I'm in a second-rate production of *Annie?*" Stephanie asked. "Dr. Rankin said they were writing Brick Preston out of the show, so—"

"WHAT?" I sat bolt upright. Amy sprang into a crouch, as if she were about to lunge at Stephanie's throat.

"So he's going to finish high school," Stephanie went on, unruffled, "and then decide whether to go on to college, or back to acting."

I tried to clear my head, which seemed to be stuffed with a mixture of cotton candy and bathtub grout. Brick Preston (in reality, Thad Marshall) was going to be in *my* high school. Maybe sitting in *my* classroom.

For months I had dreamed of Brick at night, fantasized about him during the day, and seen his face every time Rob kissed me. And now the dream was coming true.

7

I would meet Brick Preston (Thad Marshall, of course), in real life. We would get to know each other—very quickly. And then I would gaze into his dark, brooding eyes as he confessed that he'd fallen hopelessly, madly, incurably in love with me.

"What should I wear tomorrow?" Amy was wondering. "Ohh, I haven't anything to *wear.*"

"I don't see that it makes a difference," Stephanie said, "considering that three hundred other girls are going to be throwing themselves at him so hard they'll bounce off. You probably won't even get near him without stepping over a pile of bodies."

I myself had no qualms about vaulting over three hundred prostrate teenagers if that's what it would take to initiate the truly meaningful relationship that Brick and I would have. It seemed like a minor hurdle to someone who was prepared to climb the highest mountain and swim the deepest ocean if Brick wanted me to.

"Look at Kate," Stephanie said. "You don't see her getting all silly and hysterical, do you? You *are* all right, aren't you, Kate?"

"I'm perfectly fine," I said. "I'm still resting."

"Katie isn't as calm as she looks," Amy said knowingly. "Inside she's churning with emotion."

Stephanie smiled her most condescending smile. "Katie, are your insides truly churning with emotion?"

"Certainly not." What a lie. My insides had churned enough in the last twenty minutes to turn the milk of human kindness into butter. "You did say tomorrow, didn't you, Steph?"

Rob picked me up the next morning, just as if it were a perfectly normal, ordinary school day. I slid into the front seat of his 1969 Dodge Dart and slammed the door. I opened it and slammed it again. The third time, it closed.

"You going to get that fixed?" I asked automatically.

"Don't pick on my car. It runs great." We'd been following this script for four months. It was a ritual by now. I wondered if Brick would bring an entirely new script with him. . . . I allowed myself a pleasant little shiver, and my palms began to leak.

Rob threw me an affectionate glance before he wrestled the gearshift from Drive to Reverse and backed the Dart out of our driveway. His blue eyes were calm and untroubled. He didn't look like his insides had ever churned with emotion.

I'd been going with Rob for four months. I don't even know how it started exactly. We'd been friends for a long time, and then, somehow, we got to be better friends. Closer. Everyone assumed that we were seeing each other exclusively. We were, but that might have been simply because neither one of us was particularly interested in anybody else.

And our friends thought we made a perfect couple. Rob is a good student, has the brain of a rocket scientist and will probably be one. I'm no rocket scientist, but my parents think I have a talent for logical thinking and argumentation. We each have a good sense of humor, though Rob is more likely to laugh at a joke than to tell one.

And we both like classical music, which, to three-fourths of our friends, indicates that we share a bizarre and exotic inclination, and were therefore meant for each other.

Not that I didn't like going with Rob. I liked talking

to him, being with him, studying with him. But it was the kind of relationship that—well, when we told our parents we were doing our homework together, we actually did our homework. When I didn't soar to heights of grand passion when he kissed me, I figured maybe I wasn't ready for soaring yet. Sixteen might be a little young for soaring.

But then came *Lonely Days, Restless Nights*. And Brick. Within two days I realized that sixteen was not too young—grand passion-wise.

I didn't stop seeing Rob—but when we kissed, visions of Brick Preston danced behind my closed eyelids. I knew—with that keen legal mind my parents are so proud of—that Brick was a fantasy lover and Rob was the real, the here-and-now, the normal.

But that was just it. The fantasy was so much more intriguing than the reality.

Rob's car burped its way up School Street. I looked out the window. Some watery sunshine filtered through the February gloom for a moment.

"It's a sign," I said, without thinking.

"What's a sign?" Rob asked.

"The sun. It means better times are coming, things are looking up, there's a rainbow round the corner, all that stuff." Quick thinking. What I'd really meant was that maybe the sunshine was a good omen for Brick and me, a sign that our romance would flourish, that our relationship would be fruitful and prosper. Well, prosper anyway.

We pulled into the school parking lot. The sun disappeared and the sky looked dirty again.

"I hope you don't put too much faith in signs," Rob remarked.

My mittens were so moist by this time, I thought I'd have to wring them out. I looked around for any sign of Brick—a brass band, a TV mobile unit, press photographers, rioting students, a pile of female bodies blocking the main door.

Nothing. The administration hadn't even had the class to put a WELCOME, THAD MARSHALL!! banner across the gates. But maybe it was better this way. If no one knew he was going to be here, I'd have a chance to meet Thad first, and have him fall incurably in love with me by the time word got out.

"By the way," I said, trying to make my voice sound ordinary, "did you know that Thad Marshall is starting school here today?"

"Who's Thad Marshall?"

"You know, the actor who plays Brick Preston on *Lonely Days*. For heavens' sake, you see him practically every day."

"Only when I'm at your house," he muttered. He drove past the rows of teachers' cars which took up most of the front parking area and around the side of the building to the student parking field. He didn't seem particularly excited at the idea of going to the same school as Thad Marshall. That made one of us.

We turned left behind the school and Rob brought the car to a screeching halt. "What's going on over there?"

Down toward the other end of the parking area was an enormous mob of kids, milling around crazily. It looked as if the entire population of North was staging a riot. Kids were climbing over the hoods of parked cars, standing on the tops of the cars and shouting, or bobbing up and down to see over other kids' heads. A number of girls were perched on male shoulders, like children at a parade, waving their arms wildly.

Everybody was yelling.

Rob inched the car toward the mob. There were cars backed up behind us and no way to turn around.

"Why is everybody—"

"I told you," I said. "Thad Marshall is coming. He must be here already."

"You'd think it was the President," Rob said.

"The President wouldn't draw this big a crowd."

We managed to find a parking space halfway down the row. We climbed out of the Dart and slammed the doors—four or five times.

"You want to see what's going on?" Rob asked.

I hesitated. Did I want to join that wild mass of gawking, screaming kids? Could I watch them tear—God forbid—Thad's clothes off? Did I want Thad's first glimpse of me—assuming he could glimpse me at all—to be as a participant in a mad, mindless public orgy?

"You want to see him?" Rob asked. "Or what?"

What a silly question. Of course I wanted to see him. But not like this, not as one of his frenzied fans. I wanted to see him in private, say at a small, candle-lit restaurant. He would lean across the table and take my chin in his hand and trace my lips with his finger, just as he'd done with Brooke, and a violinist would play the love theme from Tchaikowsky's *Romeo and Juliet* as our Asparagus Hollandaise congealed. "You're so different from all the others, Kate," he would murmur. "All those silly, screaming teenagers . . ."

I held back another moment, my eyes closed, my

breathing shallow, my mittens moist. *"Yes,"* I said finally. "I want to see him."

But by that time Thad Marshall was completely surrounded. I assumed it was Thad Marshall who was in the middle of the crowd—actually, I couldn't tell. Rob and I wound around the fringes of the rioters, unable to catch the merest glimpse of him.

As the mob surged toward the school entrance, we straggled along, while two hundred kids shouted, screamed, shoved, waved pieces of looseleaf paper, and generally made fools of themselves.

What a letdown. Even if this hadn't been the way I'd wanted to meet Thad, I'd still wanted to see him. Just for a moment, just long enough for our eyes to meet across a crowded crowd, just long enough for our hearts to quicken, our souls to recognize their mates.

We walked up the front steps and through the main doors into the school. The crowd had re-formed itself outside the main office.

"I suppose we could stand here with everyone else and wait till he comes out," Rob said, with a notable lack of enthusiasm.

"If I were him," I said, "I'd never come out."

By lunchtime I still hadn't seen Thad Marshall, though it seemed as if everyone else in the school had. He was all they talked about, anyway. I was frustrated and depressed. Thad Marshall had not only come out of the office, but, apparently, been everywhere—except for wherever I was. There were only three periods left after lunch—only three more chances for Thad to be in one of my classes.

13

I had just sat down at a table when Amy came rushing toward me, flushed and breathless. She dropped her books and nearly fell onto the bench.

"He's—he's—you're not going to believe this."

"Try me," I said glumly.

"He's in my class. Chemistry. Just now. I mean, I just left him this *minute.* I can't stand it. I'm going to *die.*"

"In *your* class?" Wait a minute, that's not the way it's supposed to be!

Amy began to pull stuff out of her bag: lipstick, mirror, comb, brush, tissues, hand lotion, blusher. She gave a little shriek as she looked in the mirror. "God, I look *disgusting!* He *saw* me looking disgusting." She began to repair the damage.

"Then why bother with all that now?" I said nastily.

"He might have lunch this period." She brushed her slightly damp honey-colored hair while twisting her head back and forth to scan the cafeteria. At any moment she was liable to poke herself in the eye with her brush. If I didn't do it first.

I made a valiant effort to suppress my jealousy. I am a decent, moral person, I reminded myself, vitally concerned about my fellow human beings. I am a loyal, devoted friend. I am happy when good things happen to others, not jealous; I take pleasure in my friends' joys and share in the bitterness of their sorrows. I am kind to animals.

I was well on my way to convincing myself that my elevation to sainthood was only a matter of time when I remembered how lousy Amy was in chemistry. She will probably, I thought, blow Thad up before I even get a chance to meet him.

"You should have been there," Amy said.

You're telling *me?*

"All the kids were mobbing his table. Liza Mansfield *sat* on it and played with his pen." Amy sounded outraged. I knew just how she felt.

"It took Mrs. Rosen ten minutes to get everybody away from him. Some of those kids weren't even in our class."

Amy was still swiveling her head back and forth in hopes of spotting Thad. There were a million questions I wanted to ask her. What's he like? Is he as gorgeous in person as he is on TV? Did he like it when Liza Mansfield played with his pen? Will you be doing any dangerous experiments in chemistry this week?

But suddenly Amy turned to me, all wide-eyed and trembly. "Kate, what if I get him for a lab partner? Oh, God, I'll be so nervous I'll die, I know I will."

All thoughts of noble character, impending sainthood, the bonds of friendship were forgotten. My voice was cold and menacing. "If you blow him up," I warned, "I will kill you."

I was not in the best of moods when I walked into my Math 11 class, the last period of the day. The entire world had seen Thad Marshall. Regiments of high-strung, hard-breathing girls were marching through the corridors of North High School triumphantly flourishing autographs.

Autographs, for heavens' sake. How tacky. And how unfair! Why did fortune smile upon these frivolous, immature, unworthy people, while I, *truly* in love—hopelessly, madly, incurably in love—was to be denied my destiny? *It's not fair!* I very much wanted to whine.

15

But the minute I walked through the classroom door, I knew fortune had smiled on me after all. Even a person far less observant than I, without my keen legal mind, would have noticed that something unusual was going on.

About twenty-five kids were clustered around a desk in the back row, which was not visible because of the twenty-five kids clustered around it. They were elbowing and shoving each other, trying to get closer to the desk. Mr. Gelber stood in the front of the room, his face turning a rich shade of purple.

"Let's settle down, folks. Uh, let's settle down."

Nobody paid the least bit of attention to him. Mr. Gelber is a very nice, very young teacher who wants us to like him. He never raises his voice.

Settling down was a good idea, I thought, since my legs were beginning to weaken anyway, so I slid behind my desk and dropped my books on the floor beneath it. I suddenly felt an urgent need to fan myself.

As soon as those idiots sit down, I thought, I'm going to see him. I'm going to turn around, very casually, just like I was sort of looking around the room, and see him at last. I'll smile—just a friendly, reassuring smile. Sort of a private signal. Not everybody in this school has gone totally berserk, my smile will say. And he'll smile back. And later, after class, when everyone leaves . . .

I rummaged in my bag for a tissue to dry my palms.

I was saying, I will be calm, I will not go berserk, to myself for the third time when Mr. Gelber finally gave up trying to be nice. Mr. Gelber screamed.

"SIT DOWN AND SHUT UP OR I'LL START KNOCKING HEADS!"

There was sudden, total silence. For a minute everyone froze. Mr. Gelber had never been known to scream, let alone knock a head.

Then they scattered.

My moment had come. I turned slowly around as the mob cleared away. At last I could see Thad's desk.

Liza Mansfield was sitting on it. She slid off—actually, she sort of oozed off—and I finally got my first look at Thad Marshall, in person.

Now I knew perfectly well that real life hardly ever lives up to fantasy—after all, hadn't three months of watching *Lonely Days* proven that to me? So I was fully prepared—well, partly prepared—just in case Thad Marshall didn't look a bit like Brick Preston. Just in case he was, in fact, plain, unsinister, mild-eyed, and dressed in a button-down shirt.

I was not fully prepared to find out that the Thad Marshall sitting in my Math 11 class looked almost *exactly* like Brick Preston, even with no makeup, no leather jacket, and no TV lighting. (He was wearing a button-down shirt.) His hair (definitely his own) didn't look as dark as it did on television, but other than that, he was the Brick Preston of my dreams, the dark hero of my fevered fantasies. He was frowning—just like Brick—and I thought he looked tired.

Who could blame him? It can't be very pleasant to have kids shouting and clutching and swarming all over you for seven hours, to sign hundreds of autographs, to have Liza Mansfield perch on your desk every time you sat down.

Although, in the case of Liza Mansfield, I could see how a boy might not find her desk-perching entirely repulsive.

And then, just as I'd imagined, our eyes met.

17

Well, not exactly as I'd imagined. I forgot my reassuring smile, I forgot our little private signal, I forgot everything, except that I was looking into the eyes of my soulmate.

My soulmate was still frowning. His dark eyes gave no indication that they recognized the love of his life, his destiny, the woman for whom he'd been searching these past eighteen (nineteen? seventeen? I had no idea how old he was) years.

He shifted his gaze, his eyes moving from mine to focus on the blackboard. That's when I realized I'd been staring at him. For a long time.

My cheeks were hot as I turned abruptly toward the front of the room. Stupid! Now Brick would think I was like all those other kids, like all those other hysterical fans.

Well, wasn't I?

No! I had never shrieked, gawked, or drooled over a show biz idol in my life. While they had flitted from star to star, ready to pin their fickle affections on the next pretty/rugged/sexy face that flashed on the screen, I had saved myself for him. My love had never been diluted, had never been dissipated in minor-league crushes on lesser luminaries. In fact, I hadn't even known what love was until I saw Brick Preston.

". . . no more of this nonsense," Mr. Gelber was saying. "This is a classroom, not a zoo. Pass your homework down and open your books to page ninety-four."

Why couldn't I be sitting behind Thad? I would hand him my homework to pass, our fingers would accidentally touch, a spark of electricity would pass through our fingertips. He would slowly turn around and . . .

18

Someone jabbed at my shoulder.

"Kate, take this, will you?" Kenny Greco, who sat behind me, shoved some papers over my shoulder. I didn't even turn around, just reached my arm back and took the homework. Our fingers touched. Big deal.

I tried to concentrate on algebra, on what Mr. Gelber was explaining, on how important it was to pass this course if I wanted to get into the college of my choice and be accepted to Harvard Law, where I would edit the *Law Review* and finish first in my class.

But I began to imagine that Thad was staring at the back of my head, his dark eyes hot with desire. Maybe he had looked away before not because I'd been staring, but because the intensity of his emotional reaction to me had been so strong that it had shocked him. And now, when he could do so safely, he was gazing at the back of my head, his heart filled with hope and longing.

But what if Thad wasn't staring at the back of my head out of a sudden, unexpected surge of passion, but because Kenny Greco had done something outrageous to my hair with Scotch tape and paper clips?

I started to feel not only dazed, but self-conscious. For most of the period I was edgy with the effort of not smoothing my hair down, or otherwise checking to make sure that the back of my head didn't look weird.

By the time the period ended, I was exhausted.

I hadn't heard one word Mr. Gelber had said.

The bell rang. Twenty-five kids leaped to their feet and converged at Thad's desk.

"OUT!" Mr. Gelber yelled. He charged toward the mob, eyes flashing, brows lowering. "Out of this room! Get to your homerooms! NOW!"

Liza Mansfield didn't even have time to push her way to Thad's desk, let alone assume a perch. Mr. Gelber waded into the crowd and began to do some serious dispersing.

I slowly got to my feet. The other kids, realizing that Mr. Gelber meant business, reluctantly began to leave.

"And don't stand in front of that door!" he shouted. "Go straight to your homerooms!"

Slowly I gathered my books together. I had to rearrange them a couple of times to make sure the pile was properly balanced. It's very bad for your posture to walk with a stack of unbalanced books in your arms. You can put a terrific strain on your pelvis and other vitally important areas if you're not careful how you carry heavy loads.

I was *very* careful. It took me a while to get the books stacked exactly right. By that time, through some fortunate coincidence, the area around Thad's desk was entirely clear.

I smoothed my hair down in the back. Kenny Greco had apparently not done anything outrageous to it. This was it. The moment I'd been waiting for. The class was over, the room was almost empty.

I would smile at him, like I'd wanted to before. An encouraging smile, just to let him know I understood how he felt about me—and I liked it.

I took a deep breath and turned around. Thad stood up. He pushed his chair back and picked up an enormous stack of textbooks. He didn't seem to be concerned about straining his pelvis. He just scooped up the pile any which way and began walking toward me.

I forgot to smile. I think I forgot to breathe. Thad flashed a sort of rueful little grin at me and walked quickly to the front of the room and out the classroom door.

Mr. Gelber's homeroom kids were just coming in. There was a good deal of shrieking and squealing as Thad tried to get past them.

Mr. Gelber's face was just starting to turn a mottled red when I stumbled out of the room.

Three

HE'D *SMILED* AT me. He'd smiled at *me*.

I hadn't stopped replaying the scene for ten minutes.

Now, in Rob's Dart, I could still see the look on Thad's face, still feel the warmth of his personality radiating toward me, still feel the rush of panic that had made me forget my own smile plan.

However, getting out of the school parking lot is never easy, what with everyone else trying to get out of the school parking lot at the same time, and the whimsical reverse gear on Rob's car, so the prospect of imminent death did begin to loom a little larger than Thad Marshall's smile. At least, for the moment.

Rob was struggling with the gearshift, which he could not wrestle from Reverse to Drive.

"Rob," I asked nervously, "are we going to have to ride all the way home in Reverse again?"

"No, it'll shift in a minute. I just have to get over that bump."

"*Rob*—" We were driving backward in a stream of traffic, facing the line of cars going forward.

"Don't panic. Just tell me if anything happens in front of us."

"Which way is in front of us?" I cried. Rob's head was twisted around toward the rear window. I figured that meant he wanted me to look out through the windshield, but what I was supposed to watch for I wasn't sure. What I saw was a guy in the car behind us (in front of us?) making extremely rude gestures at me.

We went slowly over the bump and kept moving backward.

"There!" he said triumphantly. He shifted into Drive and turned right around the row of cars heading for the exit. He inched back into the line of traffic.

I exhaled. "You know, all the charm has gone out of this car, Rob. At first I thought it was just kind of quaint, but it's wearing thin. This car is a death trap."

"It runs great," Rob said cheerily.

"Backwards!" I yelled. "It runs great backwards."

I settled back against the seat. My mind relatively clear, I could concentrate once again on Thad.

Why had I thought Thad looked rueful? Was he sorry he couldn't stop and talk to me? Maybe that was it. It was sort of a grin of regret, a smile that said, "I really did want to meet you, and yes, I certainly did feel that spark of electricity between us the moment our eyes met, but if I don't get out of here I'm going to be trampled to death."

On the other hand, was I sure it was regret in his smile? Maybe it was just tiredness. After all, he must have been exhausted. He'd been mobbed and pestered and groped at all day long, while he was just trying to be a normal high school student and concentrate on learning algebra. It might be hard to concentrate on

23

algebra with Liza Mansfield sitting on your desk and playing with your pen.

Why hadn't I smiled back? I'd just meant to be sympathethic and reassuring, but if Thad happened to fall madly in love with me on the spot, I could have handled that too.

At least, I'd thought I could. As it turned out, I couldn't even handle sympathy and reassurance, let alone love at first sight.

But tomorrow's another day, I reminded myself, and another algebra class. I have another chance, and if Thad doesn't realize till tomorrow afternoon that he's putty in my hands, well, what's one more day measured against a whole lifetime of ecstasy?

Rob was saying something, but I don't know what it was. After I began thinking of a whole lifetime of ecstasy, I didn't pay much attention to anything. . . .

We got to my house just in time for the beginning of *Lonely Days, Restless Nights*. I turned on the TV in the den and we sat down on the couch to watch.

For the first five minutes of the show, nothing much happened. That is, Brick wasn't on the screen.

"This is really a stupid show," Rob said.

"I know."

"So why do we watch it?"

I don't know about you, but I know why *I* watch it.

"Because we have very bad taste?" I suggested.

Rob kissed me. "You taste pretty good."

Even as he said it, I heard Brick Preston's voice. We both turned to look at the set.

"Allison, calm down," Brick was saying. "Whatever it is, it can't be that bad."

24

They always say that on this show. They're always wrong.

"Oh, Brick, I had to see you. I knew I shouldn't come. I tried not to. But I couldn't help myself."

I knew just how she felt.

"Then don't try so hard," Brick said softly.

Rob began to run his fingers through my hair.

"But we have to be so careful," Allison said.

Brick slid the mink coat off her shoulders and let it drop to the floor. Allison's eyes were wide, almost fearful. It's possible—though not probable—that she was worried about her coat. Brick looked down at her for a long moment. Then he wrapped his arms around her.

Rob began to dot my cheek with gentle little kisses.

Brick's voice grew urgent. *"Allison . . ."*

I was an ice cream cone in the July sun. Whether it was Rob's kisses (which didn't usually affect me like this) or Brick's voice, or Rob's kisses combined with Brick's voice, all I knew was that in one more minute I was in serious danger of melting.

Brick gave Allison a searing kiss.

Rob gave me a searing kiss.

Life imitates art, I thought dopily, or is it the other way around? I could almost see the numbers flash by as my blood pressure zoomed upward.

"Allison," said Brick, "I—"

"Brick, I—"

"Rob, you—"

"Pay no attention to the man in the kitchen with the Cheese Doodles," my father called.

Rob let go of me abruptly and jumped up. He cleared his throat. Several times. Maybe he was getting

25

a cold. I sank back against the couch and waited for my blood pressure to go down.

"We were just—uh—"

Poor Rob. Maybe he's getting laryngitis too. I gazed at the screen. The Kraft Kitchen people were doing something bizarre with cheddar cheese and miniature marshmallows.

"Just fooling around," my father finished. "I understand. Even Kate's mother and I have been known to kiss on special occasions."

"Well—uh—"

Poor Rob. A speech impediment too. "I mean, don't worry. We—um—"

"I'm not worried," my father said. "Dylan just got home."

Sure enough, Attila came bounding into the den, saw Rob, shrieked with delight, and flung himself toward the couch. Rob fell back with a grunt and Dylan climbed onto his shoulders.

"Well, back to the salt mines," my father said. "Have fun, you three."

My father and mother are architects and their office is a wing they built off the kitchen. Usually I can hear their door open from the office into the house. Somehow I hadn't noticed it today.

"We're watching this show," Rob said, "so you have to be very quiet, okay, Dylan?"

"Okay." The Littlest Hun bounced up and down on Rob's shoulders.

The commercial was over. The next scene was in a hospital where Brooke was lying in bed, staring blankly at a wall.

Since Brick wasn't in this part, I stared fairly blankly

at the television set, trying to figure out why it was I'd nearly melted a few minutes ago. Was it Rob's kissing or Brick's kissing? If Rob had kissed me, without Brick's voice in the background, would I have had the same reaction? I never had before. But Rob hadn't indulged in many searing kisses before either. And what about Thad? I mean, it was Brick Preston I was in love with.

But Thad *was* Brick. Brick was Thad. It was terribly confusing. Even my keen legal mind couldn't figure it out.

"What's the matter with her?" Dylan pointed to the TV.

"She's got amnesia," Rob said.

"What's amnesia?"

"She forgets things."

"I forgot my lunch money today," Dylan said, "and I'm not in the hospital."

"You will be if you don't stop thumping on my head," Rob said.

It was such a weird feeling. I had seen Thad Marshall in person just an hour ago, and while I watched him on television, I didn't think of him as Thad Marshall-in-my-math-class at all. It was like they were two separate people. Well, of course they were. One was a character, and one was an actor. But while Thad was acting Brick, I hadn't even remembered he was Thad.

And when Thad smiled at me, had I been thinking of him as Thad or Brick? Brick hardly ever smiled, so I think I saw him as Thad, but how could I be sure? After all, it was Brick Preston I'd fallen in love with, not Thad. But it was Thad Marshall who was in my algebra class, not Brick.

27

For once I was glad Dylan was around. Between trying to watch *Lonely Days* while keeping Dylan from kicking him in the chest, thumping on his head, and sliding off his shoulders, Rob's fingers were far too busy to go walking through my hair.

One thing was clear. Whether I was madly in love with Brick, or Thad, or both, it could not have been Rob's kisses alone that provoked that feeling of instant melting. In the four months that we'd been going together I had never required the services of a blood pressure specialist.

What had happened, I gradually realized, was that with my eyes closed, and my lips puckered, I had disappeared from our den, and been magically transported to Brick's apartment, where my fur coat had slipped off my shoulders as easily as I had slipped into Allison's role.

I heard my name and looked up.

". . . don't want Allison to learn the truth," Brick was saying menacingly.

That's not my name, I told myself. Kate is my name. And that boy blackmailing Bill is in my math class. I held my hands together tightly, as if I could get a grip on myself that way. I got dents in my palms, but I didn't feel any less confused.

"What's blackmail?" Dylan asked.

"Shh!" I leaned forward to hear.

"It's when you pay someone not to tell something," Rob explained.

"Like if I saw you and Katie making out, you'd give me a dollar not to tell?"

"That's not worth a dollar anymore," Rob said drily.

By the time the show was over, I was exhausted. The

only straight thinking I was capable of was resolving never to watch *Lonely Days* with Rob again. It was going to be hard enough to keep things sorted out now that I was going to see Brick (Thad) in person every day and wait for him to fall madly in love with me. The last thing I needed was to have Rob watch me watch Brick on TV.

It was at this point, with my head spinning, my senses reeling, my grasp on reality slipping, and my keen legal mind shredding to coleslaw, that I began to suspect that I might not graduate first in my class at Harvard Law.

Four

THAD MARSHALL WAS not in Mr. Gelber's room the next day when I took my seat. I wondered if yesterday's experience with the lunatic element of North had given him second thoughts about finishing high school.

How terrible that would be, I thought, how awful for poor Thad, never to finish high school, never to go on to college, never to have the chance to find out if he could have been a doctor or a writer or a hotel management trainee. To be stuck all his life, playing love scenes with glamorous but shallow actresses, attending tedious Academy Award ceremonies, posing endlessly for *People* magazine, never realizing that for one brief moment, love had beckoned to him in an algebra class.

I had almost convinced myself I was sorry for Thad, not me, when the bell rang and he entered the room.

Everyone turned to watch as Thad walked quickly to his desk and sat down.

I wondered if this had been planned. Maybe Thad made an arrangement with the principal to hole up someplace (where? a broom closet? which one?) until the halls were clear. It seemed like a sensible thing to do, I supposed, but it might very well louse up the course of true love; it was going to be difficult for Thad to recognize me as his soulmate if he never saw anything of me except the back of my head in algebra.

Mr. Gelber announced there would be a quiz to see if we had understood yesterday's lesson and the homework.

What homework?

I looked, mystified, at the problems on the board and told myself that this was just a sort of diagnostic quiz. It probably wouldn't count very much.

Besides, maybe I could fake it.

Unfortunately, math doesn't seem to be one of those subjects you can fake. Numbers are so rigid, and you never get any extra credit for style.

When the time was up I handed in my paper. My name was at the top—and there was a lot of blank space underneath it.

A few minutes before the bell rang, Thad got up and walked out of the room. Mr. Gelber nodded at him and I was sure that some sort of plan had been worked out to alleviate mass hysteria and general uproar.

Ill-starred lovers, I thought, just like Romeo and Juliet. Everything was conspiring against us. If I never even got a minute alone with Thad, how could our romance be kindled, how could it flourish, then blossom into grand passion, followed by a lifetime of ecstasy?

In fact, how was Thad even going to know that we *had* a romance?

I heard the murmured comments of my classmates as

the door closed behind Thad. Kenny Greco leaned over my shoulder and whispered, "No mingling with the commoners, right, Katie?"

"Yeah, right," I muttered.

But I hoped he was wrong. Because if Thad never indulged in even a modicum of mingling, the grandest passion since Scarlett O'Hara and Rhett Butler was going to go right down the tubes.

Later that afternoon, as I watched Brick comfort Allison on our nineteen-inch (diagonally measured) color TV screen, I began to feel as if my life had been shot entirely in black and white.

I wondered when they would kill Brick off. Stephanie had said they were writing him out of the script, so I assumed Brick would die, probably at the hands of one of the innumerable women he had used like paper towels. Brick deserved to die, I suppose, if anyone really deserves to die. He was a thoroughly unscrupulous person with the manners of a jackal and the morals of a fruit fly and I would miss him terribly.

After all, Brick Preston seemed a lot more real to me on television than Thad Marshall did in person. Even though there was no glass barrier between us in Mr. Gelber's class, there might as well have been. And when Brick disappeared from *Lonely Days,* when the screen was cluttered with all the witnesses who would appear at the trial (of course, there'd be a trial, just as soon as they finished with Allison's mother's trial), my life would be totally without love. No Brick, no Thad— at least, not the way things were going in school—just leftover daydreams and faded fantasies. And Rob.

32

Rob. I felt a little twinge of guilt.

It's probably because of the algebra quiz, I told myself, and the dire effect a zero would have on my average.

Since a lifetime of ecstasy did not seem to be my destiny, I decided I might as well do my math homework.

Rob called the next morning to tell me he was taking his car to be fixed and wouldn't be able to drive me to school.

"What? Get it fixed? When it runs so great?"

"You know, Kate, you have a real sarcastic streak in you that I never noticed before."

"I've got a lot in me you never noticed before."

"What?"

"That's okay," I said. "I never noticed it before either."

"What are you talking about?" Rob sounded exasperated.

My mother stumbled into the kitchen, her hair wild, her eyes half-closed. She wore a blue sweat shirt that came down to her knees and fuzzy slippers. She groped for the coffeepot.

"I can't talk about it now; my mother's here." I hung up.

My mother took her coffee to the table and folded herself into a chair. "What can't you talk about in front of your mother?" she mumbled. "You can talk about anything to your mother."

I sat down next to her. "Good," I said, "because I have a hypothetical question to ask you. It's not about

33

me," I added hastily, "it's just a hypothetical question. . . . Let's say there's this friend of mine who's a little confused."

My mother stared into her coffee cup as if hypnotized. I wasn't sure she was awake.

"Are you listening?"

She snapped her head back, startled. "Oh, sure. Hypothetical question. Ask."

"This—um—friend of mine has to choose between two boys and it's really driving her crazy."

My mother clucked sympathetically. "Poor baby."

"Right. Anyway, one is very nice but she—uh—she doesn't—I mean, it's sort of tame."

"She doesn't hear bells," my mother said.

"That's it exactly!" I cried. "No bells."

My mother nodded. "The other one, there's bells."

"Right."

"So what's the problem? I go with the bells every time. Hypothetically speaking, of course." She took a long swallow of coffee. It didn't seem to do a thing to perk her up.

"The problem is that she's already going with boy number one, and boy number two doesn't know she's alive. Hardly. And if boy number two finds out she's alive, what about boy number one?"

My mother sagged visibly. "Kate, why are you doing this to me at this hour of the morning?"

"A little confusing, huh?"

"*I'm* beginning to hear bells," she said. "Maybe we can talk about it tonight."

"That's okay," I sighed. "Forget about it. It's not all that important." Especially since boy number two would probably *never* find out I was alive.

Anyway it had been silly of me to try and talk about Brick and Rob with my mother. I mean, I really can talk to her about anything, and she gives very good advice when I ask for it, but after all, she's been married to my father for twenty years.

What does she know about grand passion?

There was a big, red "0" on my algebra quiz. Mr. Gelber had scrawled, *"What happened to you? See me at 2:30."* across the nearly blank page.

What had happened to me was nothing I could explain to Mr. Gelber—I couldn't even explain it to my own mother—but I was sure he'd let me take the test over. I'd read the lesson and made up the homework, and I was going to concentrate on algebra for the next forty minutes, just as soon as I finished watching Thad walk to his desk. He was wearing jeans and a fisherman's sweater. He looked much more respectable than Brick. I wasn't sure how I felt about that.

I concentrated on algebra for the next thirty-five minutes, and then watched Thad walk down the aisle and out of the room. He looked good even from the back.

Rob was waiting for me at my locker after homeroom.

"Got to see about my car," he said. "Want to come along for the walk?"

"I can't. I have to talk to Mr. Gelber. I got a zero on the last quiz."

"Hey, that's too bad. What happened?"

"I couldn't begin to explain it," I sighed. That was the truth. There was no point in adding that I didn't want to explain it.

"You want me to wait?" Rob offered. "I thought maybe we could talk about your bizarre behavior on the phone this morning."

"No, you go see your car. I don't know how long I'll be."

"Well . . . okay," he said reluctantly. "I guess we can talk about your bizarre behavior on the phone later. On the phone."

"Right."

He messed my hair up a little and walked off down the hall.

I slammed my locker door and walked the other way down the hall and into Mr. Gelber's room. Mr. Gelber wasn't there.

But Thad Marshall was.

For a moment I couldn't move. I stood, frozen in the doorway, like a statue placed halfway in and halfway out of a room.

Then, with my legs feeling like marble statue legs, I clumped toward the nearest desk and dropped my (carelessly stacked) load of books. Mostly on the floor. (This is another danger of improper book-piling.)

Embarrassed is such an inadequate word. I stooped down hastily to pick them up, my cheeks feeling as if I'd just been for a spin in a clothes dryer. Suddenly Thad Marshall's head was level with mine and his hands were two inches away from my hands and he was gathering up my books and I was staring right at his knees.

We both reached for the same book. Our fingers touched. Electricity? With one pinky I could have lit up Buffalo for an entire week.

I started to get up. Thad started to get up. Our heads

bumped. Hard. I thought I might have a concussion. If it didn't turn out to be fatal, I would consider killing myself.

We stood up all the way and Thad put my books on top of the desk. He grinned. "That's called 'meeting cute.'"

"What?" Maybe Thad had a concussion too.

"Meeting cute. You know, like in the movies. A dippy society girl is driving home after a party and she accidentally runs over Cary Grant. That's called 'meeting cute.'"

"That's called drunk driving," I said.

Thad laughed.

I rubbed my forehead. At least, I thought, he knows I'm alive! And Cary Grant always falls hopelessly in love with the dippy society girl, doesn't he?

"Does your head hurt?" Thad asked.

"Only when I rub it."

"Then stop rubbing it."

Mr. Gelber walked in then. He asked me to wait in the hall while he spoke to Thad.

I waited outside the door, leaning against the nearest locker. My head didn't hurt so much any more and I didn't really think I had a concussion.

And even if I did, it was surely a minor price to pay for a lifetime of ecstasy. Thad must have felt that electricity between us; electricity has to go from one thing to another. It can't only go one way. At least, I don't think it can.

When Thad emerged from the room he held the door open for me and said, "Your turn." His voice was low, and his eyes seemed dark and troubled.

He looked exactly like Brick.

My shoulder brushed against his sweater as I walked by him into the room. My shoulder could have lit up Detroit.

I stood at Mr. Gelber's desk. I wondered if I was just confused because of my possible (though not probable) concussion, or if this was to be long-term confusion, extending over a lifetime of (muddled) ecstasy.

"Kate, I can't believe this paper. Is there something wrong? Are you having a problem?"

Who, me? Having a problem? I may be having a bit of difficulty distinguishing between fantasy and reality, or deciding which one I like better, but that isn't a problem, is it? I mean, no more than your ordinary schizophrenic faces every day.

"Actually, I wasn't prepared for the test. I forgot about the homework. But I did it last night. I have it in my notebook. I meant to give it to you before, but . . . something came up. . . ."

"I'm glad to hear it. I thought—well—that there might be some trouble. You never failed a test before. And a *zero*—that's not like you at all."

I'm not like me at all these days.

Mr. Gelber looked almost distressed. He really does try to be compassionate and understanding. "All right. If you have any difficulty come and see me. We'll schedule a makeup test for next week."

"Thank you." I picked up my books and walked out of the room.

Thad was waiting at the door.

"Thought you might want a ride home."

This isn't happening. Thad isn't really here. I guess I *can't* tell the difference between fantasy and reality anymore. Because this is the stuff my dreams are made of and dreams aren't supposed to come true. No matter how determined I was yesterday that Thad (or Brick) and I were destined for each other, I'm sure I didn't actually believe it. I mean, they're called fantasies because they're too fantastic to be real.

"Hey, am I making you nervous?" he asked. If this was a figment of my imagination standing in front of Mr. Gelber's door, my imagination had very good hearing. If he wasn't a figment of my imagination, if my destiny was actually loitering here in the flesh, I ought to say something to him.

"You're not—I mean, I'm not nervous—maybe a little surprised, that's all." I managed to get the words out, but it wasn't easy.

"Why are you surprised?"

"It's just—well, you know, everybody's been pestering you for days. I thought you might—I mean, everybody's making such a big fuss over you—" It sounded wrong the moment I said it.

"You mean I'm not worth all the fuss?" Thad sounded amused, not insulted. "I don't think so either. Can I drive you home anyway?"

You can take me by kayak to Quincy or Nyack, or on a slow boat to China, or even up the elevator in the World Trade Center, I thought, as long as we're together it's all right with me.

Oh, God, I was thinking in song lyrics. The next thing you knew, I'd be asking him if he said "tomayto" or "tomahto."

"Yes," I said finally. "That would be nice." I didn't trust myself to say anything longer than one syllable.

39

Five

THAD'S CAR WAS a cream-colored Jaguar. It matched his cream-colored jacket, which he'd slung over his fisherman's sweater. I slid into the passenger seat as Thad piled our books in the back.

I didn't bother putting on my mittens. It wasn't that cold, and they would just need to be wrung out again by the time I got home.

Thad put his key in the ignition. I felt almost lightheaded. I watched his hand—the same hand that had stroked Allison's shoulder, the same hand that had menaced Nicole, the hand that crumpled up women like paper towels—watched him turn the key and heard the surge of power as he brought the Jag to life.

Forget my mittens. *I'd* have to be wrung out by the time I got home.

I thought I'd better say something, before I got so focused on Brick and his love life that I couldn't concentrate on Thad. And my own.

I cleared my throat. "My name's Kate Bennett. What's yours?"

Thad looked at me for a second in disbelief. "You really *aren't* very impressed with me, are you?"

I felt my cheeks getting hot again. Suddenly I was having an awful lot of trouble just stringing simple, polite words together into simple, polite sentences.

I surreptitiously wiped my palms inside my jacket pockets. I turned my head the littlest bit to look at him without him thinking I was looking at him. His eyes were slightly squinted against the sun. His lips were parted a bit, and I imagined they were soft and firm at the same time. I thought how they must feel to Allison, and then I wasn't thinking about how Allison felt, but how I would feel with his mouth pressed against mine.

No wonder I couldn't think clearly. No wonder I was having trouble saying anything remotely sensible. I was mere inches away from a dream, minutes away from storybook romance, and maybe a week, tops, till I embarked on a lifetime of ecstasy.

Who could talk? Who could think? It was a moment to be savored, treasured, *experienced,* not a conversational gap to be hastily filled with meaningless chatter. Maybe Thad felt that way too. Maybe he understood completely why I was silent.

"How do I get to your house?"

Well, maybe he didn't. "Right at the next light and then straight for six blocks. Left on Fillmore." I managed to make my voice sound brisk and business-like. The effort nearly exhausted me.

Again there was dead silence. We turned right at the light and left onto Fillmore. I had something to say again.

"Four blocks and then right on Weeping Willow Way."

41

"That sounds like something out of Sunset Landing," he said. Sunset Landing is the town on *Lonely Days*.

"It is sort of a dumb name," I agreed, "considering the builder cut down all the weeping willows when he put up the development."

Thad smiled. I was doing better now. Encouraged, I added, "I watch your show."

"You *watch* that crap?"

"You *know* it's crap?" I blurted out.

That did it. I give up, I thought, I just give up. Grand passion pops up in my life like a beautiful wildflower and what do I do but smack it right in the petals with a wet towel. If I never embarked on a lifetime of ecstasy, I had no one to blame but myself.

He turned onto Weeping Willow Way. "Hey, listen, I'm not insulted. It's a living."

"Fourth house down," I said dully. "On the right."

"Why do you watch it?" Thad didn't really sound insulted at all, just curious.

Why do you think I watch it? I wanted to say. Why does anybody watch that show? To see Dr. Paul's acrylic toupee? To watch Brooke's blank face as she lies in the Interminable Ward? I watch it for the same reason everyone else watches it, you dummy. Because *you're* on it.

Thad pulled the Jag into our driveway and turned off the motor. "Well," he said, "why *do* you watch it?"

Was I imagining it, or did he look a little *too* amused? Maybe—a teeny bit conceited? Maybe he took it for granted that I watched the show because I had a crush on him. (Of course, it wasn't an ordinary crush, but he couldn't know that.) He probably expected any woman who looked at him to fall helplessly under his spell—

and three days at North could only have confirmed his expectations.

This smug self-assurance I thought I detected was definitely irritating. I looked him straight in the eye and said bravely, "I like the sets."

He started to laugh. I felt much better. I sensed some of my old spirit coming back. "Come on in," I added. Was there no end to my courage? "It's almost three-thirty and I don't want to miss your death scene."

If I'd thought watching *Lonely Days* with Rob's kissing me was weird, it was nothing compared to watching it with Thad sitting next to me on the couch, and Brick glowering out at me from the TV set. Talk about your double whammies. Talk about being stuck in the doorway between reality and fantasy. Talk about split personalities. I felt positively disoriented as I looked from the screen to the sofa, from Brick to Thad, from Never-Never Land to Here and Now.

At first Thad had been reluctant to watch the show with me, but I suspected he didn't want to miss it any more than I did. I had read somewhere that actors are often very uncomfortable watching their own movies, so from time to time I would glance casually over at Thad to see if he was uncomfortable.

The first commercial came after a scene where Brick erupts in a violent rage and threatens to kill Bill.

"This is such a weird experience," I said, shaking my head.

"You don't know the half of it."

"Does it bother you?" I asked curiously. "To watch yourself on TV?"

"Let's say watching you watching me watching my-

43

self is a little—strange." He shifted a few inches away from me on the couch. He really did feel self-conscious! Well, that sort of evened things up a little. Knowing that the shoe was on the other foot—or at least that we were both wearing shoes—gave me some of my confidence back.

The commercial ended. Thad turned toward the set and made a big show of concentrating on Brooke's hospital room.

"This is so interesting, Thad. There are so many things I've always wanted to know—like, for instance—um—how does it feel to do a love scene under all those hot lights with a whole lot of people standing around?" I tried to sound extremely casual.

"It feels like doing a love scene under hot lights with a lot of people watching you."

"You mean, it's nothing like real life? You don't get . . . involved?"

"Not a bit," he said firmly.

Was he trying to reassure me that kissing the actress who played Allison was just a tedious bit of drudgery that had to be tolerated, like learning lines or sitting still for makeup or posing for publicity photos?

On the screen Brooke blinked.

"Look!" I cried. "Brooke blinked!"

"I saw."

"I've been watching her lie there for a month," I said, "and this is the first time I've seen her blink. It must be awfully hard to not even twitch for so long while the camera's on you."

Brooke blinked a few more times, looking dazed. Then her mouth opened in a big O and she put her hands over it, as if she were trying to keep from screaming.

The picture got all wavy and through an electronic mist we saw a rerun of the last scene Brooke and Brick had played before Brooke got amnesia.

I remembered it well. It started out with Brooke and Brick driving recklessly along the beach road at night; it would end with Brick in one of his rages, almost killing Brooke.

I turned to look at Thad. He looked distinctly uneasy.

"Are you—um—anything like Brick?" I asked.

"That's a weird question," Thad said. "Why should I be anything like him? He's just a character in a TV show."

"But to be a really good actor—like you—don't you have to understand your character? Don't you have to know what motivates him and find some of the same emotions in yourself so you can—"

"Hey, this is a soap, not Tennessee Williams. We tape two shows a day and we have maybe a day to learn our lines. And half the time we don't even know what motivates our character because the writers don't tell us."

"Oh." I guess I sounded a little disappointed. I wasn't sure if it was because Thad had denied that he was anything like the character I had fallen in love with, or because he'd made something that always seemed so glamorous and romantic sound like a routine, nine-to-five job.

The door from my parents' office opened and was slammed shut, hard.

"Hello there! I'm making a lot of noise so I don't embarrass you!"

"Larry!" My mother's voice.

Sometimes I just hate my father's sense of humor. He'd thought I was in the den with Rob, possibly kissing. I often wonder if he takes his children seriously enough. He's the one who taught Dylan to say, when anyone asks him what he wants to be when he grows up, "A hooligan."

Thad and I stood up and turned around. I didn't want to miss the close-up of Brick that flickered on the screen, but the expression on my parents' faces made it almost worth it.

As if hypnotized, they both gazed at the TV, then shifted their eyes to Thad's face. Back to the TV, back to Thad.

My mother fixed me with a speculative frown. "Bells," she muttered. "Something about bells . . ."

I cleared my throat. "This is Thad Marshall." I pointed to the television and nearly giggled. "And *that's* Thad Marshall. My parents, Mr. and Mrs. Bennett."

"Hello, Thad," my mother said. "It's nice to meet you—both of you." My father may be a little unpredictable, but I can usually count on my mother to say the right thing. Unless she started thinking too hard about bells.

"Hi, Mrs. Bennett. Mr. Bennett. I like your house." Thad sounded *suave*. None of the boys I knew had ever sounded remotely suave. Brick wasn't suave. I wasn't sure I liked it.

"Kate told me this was a development, but your house is so unusual."

"Thank you," my father said. "We bought it when we were young and poor and redesigned it ourselves. What are you doing here? I mean, when you're *there?*"

"The show's on tape," Thad said. "I'm going to North High now."

"Well, for heavens' sake," my mother said. "Katie didn't tell us about that." She looked thoughtful again. "I don't think," she added.

"Katie isn't very impressed with me," Thad joked. "She probably didn't think it was worth mentioning."

"I'm impressed," my father said, even though he wouldn't know a soap from a sandbox. "As soon as I get dinner up we can sit down and you can tell us all about yourself."

"Larry," my mother said, "let's just put the stuff in the microwave and get back to work."

What a good idea. And leave Thad and me alone again, so that maybe the next time you walk in, trying not to catch us kissing, you will.

"Actually," Thad said, "I have to get going now anyway. I found out I'm behind in all my subjects, and I was expecting to graduate in June. I have a lot of work to do to catch up."

"Aren't you going to be acting anymore?" my mother asked.

"Not for a while. My character dies Friday, so I thought this would be a good time to make a decision about college."

Friday! That was tomorrow. Only one more day with Brick. How terrible.

The front door slammed. Attila stamped down the hall and into the kitchen. He stared at Thad. "You're not Rob. I thought Rob was here."

My father cleared his throat loudly. My mother yanked open a drawer and rummaged for something. Dylan stamped out of the kitchen, back down the hall and up the stairs. The Littlest Hun hits and runs.

"So long, everyone. It was nice to meet you," Thad said. He still sounded suave. Well, he was an actor; maybe he'd learned how to ad-lib his way through life.

I walked him to the door.

"It's been really interesting," he said.

Interesting? What could he have possibly found interesting at my house? A chatty father? A bratty brother? *Me*?

"I enjoyed meeting you all. I really did."

"Even Attila?"

"Attila? Oh, your brother. Yeah, even him. It's nice to be around normal people for a change. I like it." He smiled.

I leaned against the closet door. Weakly. He *liked* it. He likes *me*. He even likes *Dylan*. That was no more improbable than anything else that had happened this afternoon, so why question it?

He touched my cheek with his hand, lightly, just for a moment. "See you tomorrow?"

"Sure." That was about all I could manage.

"Good. Then you can tell me about Rob."

Six

I HAD COMPLETELY forgotten that Rob was supposed to call me that evening to discuss my bizarre behavior on the telephone. How could I be expected to remember anything so mundane when my cheek wouldn't stop tingling where Thad had touched it?

"Who's this?" I asked, when I answered the phone.

"It's me, Rob. Don't you know my voice by now?"

"Oh, sure, Rob." My mother looked up from her coffee and cocked her head attentively. "Sorry. I'm loading the dishwasher and I've got the phone cord stretched across the kitchen and Dylan is twanging it."

"Dylan is *what?*"

"You know. He pulls it all the way down and lets it go and it snaps back up again. Twang. Stop twanging, Dylan."

I scraped a plate, scrunching up my shoulder to hold the receiver against my ear.

"Could you maybe forget about the dishes for two minutes," Rob said, "and concentrate on me?"

"I can do both at once," I said.

"But neither one very well."

Dylan twanged on the cord again, and the receiver fell off my shoulder and into the sink. My mother grabbed him by the shirt and hustled him out of the room. She was back in the kitchen in a flash, pouring herself a third cup of coffee.

I fished the receiver out of the sink and wiped it off. "Sorry, Rob. I dropped you in the sink."

"You're doing it again," Rob said.

"Doing what?"

"Kate, I think we're having a real communication problem here."

"It's okay. Dylan's gone now."

"I don't think Dylan is the problem."

"All right, all right, I'm listening." I sat down at the table. "I'm sitting down. I'm not scraping the dishes. Go ahead and talk."

Rob exhaled loudly, right into the phone. "Forget it, Katie. I don't feel like talking now."

"No wonder we have a communication problem," I said. "If you don't want to talk why did you call?"

My mother pricked up her ears. I couldn't see her ears behind her hair, but I could tell she was pricking them.

"I *felt* like talking when I called. I stopped feeling like it when—Forget it. I'll see you tomorrow, I guess."

"Okay, if that's the way you feel about it."

"And I can't pick you up. My car isn't ready yet."

I stood up and went back to the dishwasher. The receiver was still on my shoulder. I sort of expected he'd keep on talking, even though I knew I wasn't

50

being very nice to talk to. But Rob just said, "So long," and hung up.

I frowned, and put the receiver back on the hook. My mother cleared her throat. "Thad certainly is a handsome boy," she said casually.

"He's a star. Of course he's good-looking."

I had told my parents everything there was to tell about Thad at dinner. Everything I wanted to tell, anyway.

"Rob's nice-looking too," my mother commented.

Nice looking. There it was in a nutshell. Rob is *nice* looking. He has sincere blue eyes, light brown hair, fair skin—sometimes a little chapped and pink from skiing. Medium height, medium build—medium everything. He looks healthy. Well adjusted. No danger ever lurks behind those mild blue eyes; no knowing smile ever plays about his chapped lips; there is not the slightest suggestion of dark secrets hidden in murky corners of his mind. I didn't think his mind even had any murky corners.

Whereas Brick—well, the difference was day and night.

But it was Thad my mother was talking about, not Brick. Boy, this was getting complicated. You couldn't even call it a romantic triangle, I realized. Because it's not just Rob and Thad and me. It's Rob and Thad and Brick and me. Of course, Rob was pretty annoyed with me, Thad hardly knew me—though he'd touched my cheek, that probably meant a lot more to me than it did to him—and as for Brick . . .

I was getting awfully confused.

"I have to go call Stephanie," I said.

My mother looked dejected. "This is your mother," she reminded me. "You can tell your mother anything, remember? We were going to talk about your . . . *friend's* problem tonight."

"There's nothing to tell yet," I said. "Right now I just want to talk to Stephanie. And by the way, looks aren't everything, you know."

My mother smiled benignly. "You took the words right out of my mouth."

At lunch the next day, Amy looked positively feverish. "When is he going to stop coming in late and leaving early?" she wailed. "How is a person supposed to meet another person if he's never around to meet her? I mean, if he wants to be an ordinary high school kid just like all us other ordinary high school kids, how come he avoids us all the time?"

"Maybe we don't want him to be an ordinary high school kid," I said. "Maybe we won't let him. Look how crazy everybody acted the first day he was here."

"That was two days ago," Amy said. "Everybody's calmed down by this time."

I don't know about that. I certainly haven't.

Last night, on the phone, Stephanie and I had debated the wisdom of telling Amy that Thad Marshall had spent the afternoon with me. Stephanie had urged honesty as the best policy, but I wasn't sure.

"I don't want to hurt Amy," I'd said.

"She'd be more hurt in the long run if you don't tell her now," Stephanie said. "How do you think she'd feel if everyone saw her throwing herself at Thad and then she found out that you'd been seeing him all along? She'd feel like a fool."

I thought about what Stephanie had said, and it seemed to make sense. Or as much sense as you could make out of this whole situation. So here I sat, with a feverish, frustrated Amy, trying to find a way to say, "Don't bother trying to get him interested in you. I saw him first."

There were only the two of us at the table. Rob and Stephanie had lunch fourth period. In fact, I hadn't seen Rob at all today. He hadn't been waiting at my locker when I got to school and we have no classes together, since he's a senior taking advanced everything, and I'm in eleventh grade.

"Amy, there's something I have to tell you. Something really important." I ignored my lunch, which was infinitely ignore-able, and took a deep breath. "Amy, we've been friends for a long time, and I would hate for anything to come between us, but—"

Amy looked up from her soup. "What? What's the matter?"

"It's not that anything's the matter, actually, it's just that—well, I'm afraid you might be a little upset when I tell you what I have to tell you."

"Katie, what *is* it? What's wrong? Are you mad at—"

"Thad Marshall drove me home yesterday and stayed at my house for over an hour."

Amy dropped her spoon. Right into her clam chowder. Clam chowder splashed all over her sweater. She didn't even notice.

"You're kidding." Her voice was an awed whisper.

I shook my head. "I'm not kidding. And really, it wasn't anything I planned—I mean, it was just fate. A lucky accident."

"But how?" Amy's eyes were wide. "Why?"

I told her the whole story, leaving no detail omitted. Her eyes got wider and wider, and her breathing got shallower and shallower. I think she stopped breathing entirely when I told her about Thad touching my cheek.

"I would have died," she moaned. "I would have just died."

"It was touch-and-go for a minute with me too," I admitted. "Oh, Amy, I know you wanted—"

"But, Kate, it's wonderful!" Amy's face was bright with excitement. "If it can't be me, don't you know how happy I am for you?"

"You are?" What a good person Amy is, I thought. I could never be that unselfish. When she'd told me she had chemistry with Thad, I was so jealous I'd wanted to scream. And now here she was, being happy that I was contemplating a lifetime of ecstasy with the same guy she wanted.

I was almost soppy with sentiment. "You're a noble person, Amy. Do you know that? You are positively *noble*."

"Don't be silly. We're *friends*. No mere man is going to come between us." Well . . . he wasn't that mere.

"And at least," she said, her eyes narrowing in spiteful pleasure, "glitzy old Liza Mansfield won't get him. Listen, Kate, I'm dying to know. What's Thad Marshall *really* like?"

"Well, he's—uh—" I tried to think of an answer.

"Is he nice?"

Rob is nice. Thad is . . .

I was stumped. I realized that I didn't have the slightest idea what Thad Marshall was really like.

"Come on, Katie. Is he anything like Brick?"

"I just met him yesterday. I don't really know him yet."

"But he must have made *some* impression on you. Didn't he?"

"Oh, sure, of course he made an impression on me."

"Well, *how?*"

"With his hand," I said stupidly. I touched the side of my face. "Right about here."

The closer it got to eighth period, the harder and faster my heart seemed to pound. In an hour, I'll see Thad. In forty minutes, I'll see Thad. In thirty-two minutes I'll see Thad. Time was passing so slowly that I kept holding my watch up to my ear to see if it was still working. Unfortunately, I have a quartz watch and it doesn't tick, so I had to look at it every three minutes or so to make sure the minute hand was moving.

We'll talk. He'll ask about Rob—just to begin with. Then we'll talk about big, important stuff, like whether we'll live in Hollywood or New York, and should we alert the media before we elope?

I was in Ms. Riley's English class ten minutes before eighth period. Arnie Short and Linda Faye were reading from Act One, Scene Seven of *Macbeth*. Apparently Arnie conceived of Macbeth as a sort of Godfather, because he read Shakespeare's lines just like Marlon Brando playing Don Corleone.

"We will proceed no furder in dis business. He hat honored me of late, and I have bought golden opinions from all sorts of people, which would be worn now in dere newest gloss, not cast aside so soon."

His voice was deep and husky, and he mumbled a lot. Linda started to break up and couldn't make it through her next lines. The whole class was laughing. Ms. Riley said it was the most unusual interpretation of *Macbeth* she'd ever heard.

"But don't you see the parallel here?" Arnie asked. "What's the difference between Macbeth and the God-father? One's a don and one's a thane, but they're both looking to rule the biggest territory."

Hands shot up all over the room; suddenly, everyone, including Ms. Riley, was taking sides in a raucous debate. And suddenly, I began to wonder *how* Thad was going to talk to me. When? He came into class after everyone else was seated, and left class before everyone else got up. So how was he going to talk to me? He couldn't wait for me at my locker, because he didn't know where my locker was, even if he was prepared to face another demonstration by his North High Fan Club. Would he drive me home? How would he find me? How would I find him?

When the bell rang, most of the class was still arguing over Arnie's hypothesis. It must have been a provocative discussion. I didn't contribute to it. I was provoked enough already.

I walked up to the third floor to Mr. Gelber's room.

I sat down in front of Kenny Greco and listened to my heart bang against my chest as I waited for Thad to come. It sounded so loud, I wondered if Kenny could hear it. If so, he was definitely going to get the wrong idea about me, and things were pretty complicated already without creating a romantic pentangle.

One more minute until the bell rang. Suddenly, I heard a burst of bright chatter right outside the door, and Thad walked in, just like any other ordinary student, except that three girls, including Liza Mansfield, were hanging on him. Almost literally. Liza was walking backward, so she could keep the full force of her smile focused on Thad.

"Look at that," Kenny said. "He decided to mingle with the commoners after all."

My heart stopped banging and went thud. *Now* is when Thad could talk to me, I thought. Now there's a chance for him to arrange to meet me later. Somehow he decided to arrive when everyone else arrives, and now I've got Liza Mansfield and her clones, Jane Prichard and Andrea O'Connor, to compete with. Now that he's met the Gold Dust Triplets, he won't even want to talk to me anymore.

Thad was smiling politely and nodding as they all moved up the row to his desk. The three girls seemed to be guiding him along like a trio of tugboats escorting a ship into harbor.

Before they got him to his desk though, Thad suddenly veered off course, sailed past two desks, and headed straight for me. He grinned. A sweet, intimate grin. A smile that told everyone—Liza Mansfield and her stooges, Kenny Greco, the whole class—and me— that there was something *special* between us.

He leaned over me, one hand on the back of my chair and one hand on my desk, and said softly, "Wait for me at the end of the period."

All I could do was look up at him with big, adoring eyes, like a cocker spaniel puppy on a cheap birthday card. I was too dumbfounded to even nod my agreement.

The class was buzzing with excitement—possibly shock. Everyone turned around to look at me—*me*, Kate Bennett, of the (formerly) keen legal mind. Liza

Mansfield and her crew were practically goggle-eyed with amazement; Liza looked as if she didn't know what hit her.

I think Kenny Greco summed it up best when he leaned over me and whispered, "Liza Mansfield's hitting on him and he's making a date with *you?* No offense," he added hastily.

Even though I was thinking along the same lines as Kenny—or maybe especially because I was—I still wanted to deck him. I turned around and glared— which at least distracted me from all those other incredulous eyes. "Didn't it ever occur to you," I said coldly, "that *some* people might be interested in more meaningful qualities than mere surface sexiness?"

Kenny seemed to think that over. But only for a second.

"No," he said.

The bell rang. Mr. Gelber closed the door and opened the class.

When the bell rang at the end of eighth period, I didn't move. Thad had told me to wait for him, hadn't he? I would wait. I folded my hands in my lap, while most of the class stampeded for the door, yelling "T.G.I.F.!"

Not everybody, though. As Thad reached my desk, Liza, Jane, and Andrea lingered in an aisle, possibly hoping their ship would come in; Kenny Greco gave no indication that he would ever leave his seat.

"I have to stay for extra help today," Thad said. "I can't see you."

I hoped my big cocker spaniel eyes wouldn't begin to water, but my disappointment must have been obvious.

"Are you doing anything tomorrow?" he asked.

"Tomorrow? Saturday?"

Kenny started to stack his books. I noticed that he too seemed to take great care in piling them together, even though he had only two to stack; he was no doubt as concerned with pelvic imbalance as I was.

"If you know of a nice place for dinner around here, I thought . . ."

A nice place for dinner! Just as I'd imagined it. An intimate little French restaurant with candlelight and a strolling violinist and Asparagus Hollandaise.

Kenny Greco whistled and shook his head. He started for the door. Mr. Gelber's homeroom kids were beginning to straggle in. One look at Thad and me and they started to giggle and chatter and poke each other like overgrown four-year-olds. At least they didn't ask us for autographs.

"Well, maybe not *right* around here," Thad said dryly.

"Huh?"

Thad scooped up my books. I got up, feeling distinctly fuzzy, and held out my arms for them.

"The restaurant," he said. "Maybe we shouldn't go someplace too local."

"No, right, not too local." I walked with him to the door and kids parted like the Red Sea to let us through. It was miraculous—not just that the waves parted—the whole situation.

"Seven o'clock okay?"

"Seven's good," I said. "Seven's fine."

Or six or nine or—

"Okay. You pick us a restaurant and I'll see you. By the way, I get killed today."

For a moment I didn't understand what he was talking about. I really am in a daze, I thought, bracing myself against a water fountain. Then I remembered *Lonely Days,* and that today was the day Brick would get killed.

"Oh, no! Already?"

"Already?" Thad laughed. "He should have bought it years ago. Take care. See you tomorrow." He squeezed my hand.

Seven

I WAS NOT prepared to deal with Rob five minutes later—I was not prepared to deal with anything—but he was waiting for me at my locker.

"My car's fixed," he announced. I thought he was trying to be casual, as if last night's conversation had never taken place. But I didn't pay very close attention, not with the picture of an intimate French restaurant in front of my eyes, and Tchaikowsky's *Romeo and Juliet* ringing in my ears. I wondered if hearing *Romeo and Juliet* was the same as hearing bells.

"You want to come with me and pick it up?" he asked. "We can test-drive it. Forward."

"Uh, gee, Rob, I can't. I have to get right home and—"

"Kate, why is everybody staring at us?"

I looked around and saw that a lot of people *were* staring as they walked by. And nudging each other. And whispering. A couple of kids said, *"Hi,* Kate," and winked; one boy said, "Hi, Rob," in a voice heavy with mock sympathy.

"What's going on?" Rob demanded.

Boy, good news travels fast around here.

"Just the usual Friday crazies, I guess." It occurred to me that I somehow had never mentioned to Rob that Thad was in one of my classes. How strange, I thought, that I forgot to tell him. Oh, well. Rob was never particularly interested in Thad anyway.

"This is not the usual Friday crazies," Rob muttered. "This is *crazy*."

I slammed my locker door and started down the hall to the stairs.

"You don't want to test-drive my car?" Rob said. "You're the one who's always complaining about it."

"I can't. I don't want to miss *Lonely Days*."

Rob stopped right in the middle of the stair landing. "You want to stay home for *that*?"

"Why are you so surprised? We always watch it."

"I only watch it because you want to. Can't you miss one day?"

Sure, I can miss one day, but not today. After today I can miss *every* day, but this afternoon—

"No. Brick gets killed today."

Rob followed me down the stairs and through the main doors. "How do you know?"

"It's common knowledge. Everyone knows Brick gets killed today."

"*I* didn't know." Rob was silent for a moment. "I'm getting the feeling there are a lot of things everybody knows that I don't."

"Don't be paranoid."

The moment I said it, I felt like a rat. Why shouldn't he be paranoid? I mean, he *wasn't* paranoid, he was right. A lot of other people did know something he didn't know, something that directly concerned him. I remembered how Stephanie had urged me to be honest with Amy, how she'd said that Amy would feel foolish if she found out that I'd become involved with Thad while she was mooning over him.

How would Rob feel? By Monday, everybody in school would know that Thad Marshall had spurned Liza Mansfield for me. They might find it a little hard to believe—who could blame them?—but that would make the gossip even wilder.

"All right," Rob said decisively, "then I'll watch with you and we can pick up the car afterward."

This was not going to be easy.

"Well, of course we *could* watch together . . ." But I didn't mean it. I didn't want to watch Brick's last show with Rob sitting next to me, distracting me, trying to kiss me, and making me feel guilty because I would rather watch a taped Brick Preston than be cuddled by a live Rob Dorsey.

". . . But I won't be able to get your car with you. I have a lot of work. Homework."

"Really." Rob eyed my math book, the only book I was carrying. "You sure look loaded down."

We walked along School Street in silence. When we reached the corner, Rob stopped abruptly. He wheeled around and planted himself in front of me, folding his arms across his chest.

"All right, Kate. I can take a hint. I don't know what I did, but you're sure making it obvious you don't want to be with me. And I'm getting tired of hanging around waiting for a kind word from you."

"Rob, I—" I'd never seen him like this, never heard him talk this way. He was always so even-tempered, so easygoing. Now his mild blue eyes were steely and his lips tightened with anger.

His behavior was so unexpected, I felt more surprised than dismayed. I hadn't meant to hurt him, I was just so completely wrapped up in Thad. I never thought Rob could be like this.

"Rob, I have to—"

"I know, I know. You have all that work to do."

"No, I mean—" I meant I had to explain. Stephanie was right about being honest with Amy, and I should have been honest with Rob, too.

"Don't strain yourself," he said. "If you ever have some time to kill, give me a call."

He crossed School Street and walked off in the opposite direction from the way I went home. I was so stunned I just stood there, staring at him till he was halfway up the block. He didn't turn around to look back.

I got home just in time for *Lonely Days*. I hadn't wanted to watch with Rob because I didn't want him to distract me, but he ended up distracting me after all, even though he wasn't sitting beside me on the couch.

As I waited for Brick's final scene, I couldn't get *our* final scene out of my mind. Starting from there, I tried to recreate the week's events, going over every contact I'd had with Rob.

Had I really treated him so badly? Had I really given him any reason to be angry with me? I had been a little abrupt with him on the phone a couple of times— actually, I hadn't just been abrupt last night, I'd been almost rude—and I'd made up a pretty poor excuse for not going with him to pick up his car today, and I'd called him paranoid when he'd reacted to all those funny looks we were getting. . . . Maybe any one of those things by itself wouldn't have been particularly significant, but when you strung them all together?

A person wouldn't have to be a rocket scientist to figure out something was up.

I had been pretty thoughtless, I concluded, but a strange sense of relief began to replace my guilt. After all, now Rob had broken us up. There was no need to explain anything. By Monday he'd know about Thad and me, and this would save us both the embarrassment of a confrontation. I wouldn't have to try and explain that Thad inspired me to heights of grand passion while Rob merely—Oh, yes, it was much better this way. For everyone's sake.

I settled back with a reasonably clear mind to watch Brick die. That was about all I got to watch Brick do, because he hardly appeared on the show at all until the last two minutes.

Finally, after a deodorant commercial, Brick's apartment flashed on the screen. The camera moved toward the sofa, where Brick lay, arms behind his head, with a cigarette drooping carelessly between his fingers. I hoped he wouldn't set his beautiful hair on fire.

I leaned forward and clasped my arms tightly around my knees. Brick was brooding. Just lying there, brooding. Oh, God, he's so gorgeous, I realized again. And *I'm going out with him tomorrow night*. Live. In person. Brick Preston.

No matter how hard I pinched myself, I couldn't believe that I wasn't dreaming.

Brick's doorbell rang. At first he didn't respond—he just kept brooding. The doorbell rang a second time. Brick unfolded his arms and sat up. He took a final puff of his cigarette and stabbed it out in the ashtray. The camera followed him as he walked toward the door. He turned the doorknob slowly.

When the door was open, the camera angle changed. Now the camera was outside the apartment, focusing on a closeup of Brick's face. There was no way to tell who had rung the bell.

"Oh, it's you," Brick said expressionlessly. "I've been expecting—"

A shot rang out. The camera pulled back slightly as Brick grabbed at his chest. I gasped, and grabbed at my own chest. Two more shots. Now Brick clutched at the doorframe, his face contorted in pain. His knees buckled and he sagged to the floor.

"You," he gasped, *"you—"* He fell forward with a strangled cry, and a gun clattered to the floor next to his head.

The music came up and the screen went dark for a moment. I closed my eyes, almost as if I had been shot, and was on the edge of eternal night. Somewhere, far away, a phone was ringing.

The show's closing credits were rolling as I stood up and groped my way to the kitchen.

"Ohh, Katie, wasn't he wonderful?" Amy gushed. "How can you stand it, sitting there calmly watching, just like everybody else, and all the time knowing that hunk is madly in love with you?"

"I don't know," I said groggily. What a terrible word, *hunk*. I hate that word. Brick wasn't just a hunk—I mean, Thad wasn't a hunk. He had lots of other qualities that were far more important than mere hunkhood. Like . . .

"What's Thad Marshall *really* like?" Amy had asked. Well, maybe I didn't know yet what all those other qualities were, but I was sure Thad had them. After all, a serious, intelligent person like me could not fall madly, hopelessly, incurably in love with just *any* hunk.

"I wouldn't say he was madly in love with me yet," I said.

But tune in tomorrow.

"Listen, if you're not doing anything," Amy said, "I could come over. I've got the car."

"Sure." I could use a little dose of reality right about now.

"By the way," I added, "Thad asked me out."

Amy screamed so loudly into the phone that I yanked the receiver away from my ear.

The moment I hung up the phone rang again.

"The rat deserved to die," Stephanie hissed.

"That rat is taking me to a French restaurant tomorrow."

"I'll be right over," Stephanie said. *"Avec* champagne."

Stephanie hadn't had any champagne handy, but she brought a flask. She kept passing it to Amy and me and we kept passing it right back.

"This stuff is poisonous," I said. "I'd rather drink Mr. Clean."

"The Cinzano was all we had in the house," Stephanie said. "My parents aren't very big drinkers."

"Don't blame your parents," Amy said. "You're the one who added the Kool-Aid. Ohh, Katie, I still can't believe *Thad Marshall* asked you for a date."

"Me neither," I said. "And it's driving me crazy. Why?"

"What do you mean, why?" Stephanie asked.

"Well, I was sitting there, watching that gorgeous hunk lying in a pool of blood—"

"It wasn't a pool of blood," Stephanie cut in, "it was a tiny streak of ketchup."

"And I couldn't figure out why he would pick me; I mean Liza Mansfield was drooling all over him. Even Kenny Greco couldn't understand it."

"Kenny Greco couldn't understand *I Love Lucy,*" Stephanie said, "let alone the mysterious workings of the human heart."

"No, come on. I mean it. After you guys called I sat here trying to think of my good points. You know, what assets do I have that would attract someone like Thad?"

"You're intelligent," Amy said. "That's an asset."

"Maybe," I said uncertainly. "But I don't know how he could tell that. I haven't been acting very intelligently lately."

"You're nice-looking," Stephanie said. "In a wholesome sort of way."

"Gee, thanks."

"Don't be so touchy. You know what I mean. You're not exactly right out of the pages of *Playboy.*"

"I'm no Liza Mansfield," I said bitterly.

"But he's not interested in Liza Mansfield," Stephanie pointed out. "He's interested in plain old you."

I scowled at her. "You're too kind."

"But that's what *you're* saying," Amy reminded me. "That's why you don't understand it. Sometimes love is a matter of—you know, chemistry. He can't explain it any more than you can; he just knows that when you bumped heads it was love at first sight."

"And besides," Stephanie added, "he's used to glamour by now. I mean, he's worked with all these beautiful women; he must realize how unimportant mere physical gorgeousness is."

"How fortunate for me."

"Oh, Katie, why don't you stop questioning the whole thing and just go and enjoy yourself?" Stephanie said. "It's a once-in-a-lifetime opportunity—your basic *Fantasy Island* scenario."

"But that's my whole point! Half the girls in school have the same fantasy. Why should mine come true? It just isn't logical."

"Love isn't supposed to be logical," Stephanie said. "Why look a gift hunk in the mouth?"

Amy giggled appreciatively.

"Because I don't know how to act," I said. "I have no idea what he wants me—"

"Don't act at all," Amy said. "Just be your own sweet self. That's the way you were yesterday, right? That's the girl he fell in love with, right?"

"I don't know!" I cried. "I don't know about anything anymore."

"Then let's discuss something really vital," Stephanie said briskly. "Like what you're going to wear tomorrow night."

Eight

SATURDAY SEEMED TO stretch on interminably. It could have been partly because I woke up at 7 A.M. and began waiting for it to be 7 P.M.

By three o'clock I had played five games of War and one game of Fifty-two Pickup with Dylan, taken him to McDonald's for lunch, listened to Beethoven's Violin Concerto, and told my parents I was going out with Thad Marshall that night. My father seemed very impressed. My mother looked smug and knowing. Stephanie had suggested a restaurant called Chez Monieu and my parents thought it was a good choice. They said "The Sneaky Gourmet" had given it four carving knives in his "Dining Out" column.

I finally decided to take a long, luxurious bubble bath, just like the movie stars do when they want to relax before a big premiere. I figured that would kill an hour or so.

I was dismayed to find that the only thing remotely resembling bubble bath we had in the house was Dylan's Mr. Bubble.

"How can I take a luxurious bubble bath in Mr. Bubble?" I wailed. "Why don't we have any bubble bath in this house?"

"Because we take showers," my mother said reasonably.

"I'll smell like a six-year-old!"

"Kate, calm down. Do you want me to go out and buy you some bubble bath? Something that will make you smell like a thirty-year-old?"

"Don't bother, don't bother," I said nobly. "I'll make do. Maybe we have some Woolite or something."

"I can't stand it." My mother rolled her eyes. "If you won't go and get it, I will. Martyrs drive me crazy."

"Oh, all right. If it'll make you happy, you can buy me some bubble bath."

"Thank you, darling daughter. Nothing would make me happier than buying you bubble bath."

She came back in half an hour and handed me a small white paper bag. Inside was a black bottle with a gold top; it looked very sophisticated.

"It's called Reckless Abandon," she said. "I couldn't resist the idea of taking a bath with reckless abandon."

"Funny, funny," I muttered. "Thanks." I unscrewed the top. "Wow!"

"It's concentrated. The saleswoman told me a little goes a long way. It better. It cost ten dollars."

"I'll pay you back," I promised. "When I have ten dollars."

"I'll wait."

I ran upstairs and prepared my luxurious bubble bath. A tiny capful of Reckless Abandon under a rush of steamy water made my head spin. The air was heavy with gardenias, jasmine, and sandalwood. The bathroom smelled like an explosion in a Chanel factory.

I climbed into the tub and settled back into bubbles that came up to my chin. I wished I had a long jade cigarette holder.

I lay there for a few minutes, dizzy with Reckless Abandon and the promise of grand passion with a side order of Asparagus Hollandaise. I was almost drowsing when Dylan banged on the door.

"Kate? Wanna play Missile Command?"

"Not now. I'll electrocute myself. Go away."

My fingers and toes were all wrinkled by the time I got out of the tub, but I hadn't killed that much time. I shampooed my hair and blew it dry. I wandered back to my room and stretched out on the bed. It was only four-fifteen.

I turned on the radio. They were playing the Liebestod from Wagner's *Tristan und Isolde*. I was on the verge of being swept away by a soaring crescendo, but Dylan threw my door open and said, "Now?"

I sat up and yelled. You have to yell to be heard over Wagner. "Are you crazy? This is some of the most beautiful love music ever written!"

"Blucchh." Dylan slammed the door behind him.

At four-thirty I started putting on my makeup. Even stepping back from the mirror to scrutinize the effect of every application of every cosmetic, even though my hands trembled slightly, it still only took me twenty minutes.

By five o'clock I was dressed. Stephanie and Amy had decided that my black wool and silk sweater and white wool skirt was the perfect intimate French restaurant outfit. With chunky silver necklace and lacy black panty hose I thought I looked at least eighteen.

I went downstairs.

"Kate, you look lovely," my mother said.

"That's Kate?" my father exclaimed hammily. "I thought some glamorous movie star had wandered into our kitchen by mistake."

"*Now* can we play Missile Command?" asked Dylan.

Thad rang the bell at seven o'clock on the dot. I opened the door and for a moment we just stood there, looking at each other. He was wearing a sweater and jacket. He looked dazzling. Rob never wore a jacket. Neither did Brick—except his leather one.

After what seemed a very long time, Thad stepped inside and pushed the door closed behind himself. He didn't take his eyes off me. No one had ever looked at me the way Thad was looking at me—with such total concentration, such complete absorption. It was as if the rest of the world had disappeared and there was nothing, no one, to focus on but me.

That was how Brick looked at women.

I was blown away.

"You look so different," Thad said as he started the car.

"I'm just wearing a skirt and sweater," I replied self-consciously. And my down coat, which should have been mink. No need to tell him I'd consulted with Stephanie and Amy for an hour and a half to find the perfect intimate French restaurant outfit. And that I'd taken twenty minutes with my makeup instead of my usual five.

"Maybe. But there's something about you . . ."

Could it be the lingering aura of Reckless Abandon?

"You look different too," I said.

"Me? I'm just wearing this plain old jacket and sweater," Thad teased.

"Well, Brick never wears jackets."

For a moment Thad was silent. I wondered if I'd said something wrong.

"And Brick doesn't go to North High," he pointed out.

"Of course not." I felt a little confused. "You do. I never saw *you* in a jacket either." This was silly. Why were we talking about trivialities? Who cared what anybody wore? When were we going to get down to basics, like making a mutual commitment to a lifetime of ecstasy?

I changed the subject. "I saw you die yesterday. I thought you were really good. Very believable."

Thad laughed. "Did you? You don't think I overdid it?"

"No, not at all. You were very convincing."

"I was just following orders."

"Does it bother you that they killed you off? Do you really want to be here, instead of acting?"

"There is no place," Thad said softly, "I'd rather be than here."

I wiped my palms inside my coat pockets. "Turn right."

Chez Monieu was only a few miles away, but Stephanie didn't think any kids from school were likely to be there. "It's not your average Saturday night hangout," she'd said.

The parking lot behind the restaurant was jammed with cars. *Somebody* was hanging out there.

"This must be a good place," Thad said. "It's crowded enough."

"The 'Sneaky Gourmet' gave it four carving knives." Why did that sound so silly when I said it out loud?

We finally had to park a block away. Thad put his arm around my shoulders as we walked to the restaurant. I wished we'd parked ten blocks away.

We had to practically shove our way past the people clustered in the small entryway.

"Did you make a reservation?" Thad asked.

"Was I supposed to?" Why hadn't anybody mentioned anything about reservations to me? What did I know about intimate little French restaurants? Not once, in all my fantasies, did I contemplate reservations.

Thad spoke to a man in a blue dinner jacket with satin lapels, and reported that we would have to wait up to two hours to get a table.

"Oh, Thad, I'm sorry. I didn't realize."

"It's not your fault. I should have taken care of it. We'll find someplace else."

But it won't be an intimate little French restaurant, I thought miserably. And it won't have a strolling violinist. Or Asparagus Hollandaise.

We pried our way back out to the street. I was so disappointed Thad must have felt it.

"Come on, Katie, we'll be adventurous. We'll ride around and find something on our own—a place the Sneaky Gourmet hasn't discovered yet."

"Okay." I tried to sound cheerful. But riding around

looking for a place to eat was not exactly the sort of adventure I'd imagined.

Only a few blocks from Chez Monieu Thad spotted a Japanese restaurant in the middle of a shopping center. "Hey, great. I love sashemi and sushi. Do you?"

"I never had any. What are they?"

"Raw fish."

Reckless Abandon can go just so far. Eating raw fish was not my idea of being adventurous; I'm not even crazy about *cooked* fish.

"But there are lots of other things you could have instead," Thad said. "You don't have to eat sushi."

For a brief moment I imagined Thad kissing me good night. A long, lingering, passionate kiss, a kiss that spoke louder than any words—of grand passion in the future, and raw shrimp in the past.

This was not working out at all the way I'd planned it.

Nine

TANAKA WAS PRETTY crowded but we got a table right away. The only problem was we didn't get any chairs. They only had Japanese-style seating, which meant we sat cross-legged on puffy mats; at least, Thad sat cross-legged. I had to sort of squat on my knees, or fold my legs sideways. You just can't sit cross-legged in a narrow wool skirt.

There were no candles. The place was as bright as daylight. There was music—from speakers up near the ceiling. It was hardly likely that a strolling violinist would wander in and start playing Tchaikowsky's *Romeo and Juliet*. Probably the most I could hope for was that the slush music station oozing from the speakers might finish playing "A Summer Place" and switch to the film score from *Seven Samurai*.

A beautiful Japanese waitress in a bright pink kimono brought us hot towels. Thad wiped his hands with the towel, so I did the same. The waitress gave us each a menu. I opened mine and studied it intently. I was grateful to have something to do, someplace to look, something tangible to hold onto, even if it was only a thin sheet of plastic.

The menu was filled with words like *yakitori, shabu shabu*, and *negima* and I didn't have the vaguest idea what anything meant. At Chez Monieu I would have had a chance—I know *boeuf* means beef, *veau* means veal, and Hollandaise means Hollandaise.

"If there's something you don't understand on the menu—" Thad said.

"I don't understand *anything* on it."

It turned out that Thad could describe almost everything I asked about. I was very impressed. I was also reluctant to choose anything, because I knew that when I did, I'd have to put down my menu and face Thad across the small wooden table. If he stared at me the way he had at my front door, I wouldn't be able to lift a chopstick.

Unfortunately, it was a small menu. Before long I ran out of things for Thad to describe. I thought he might be a little startled if I asked him to explain Coca-Cola, tea, coffee, Sanka, and ice cream, so I finally said I'd try *negima*.

The waitress wrote down our order and took away the menus. There was nothing left to study but Thad.

I looked across the table. Thad was studying me.

Don't panic, I told myself, as I panicked. Think of what Allison would do when Brick gazes at her this way. Allison would begin to stammer and blink rapidly and develop a quiver in her lower lip. That was easy. I was already doing a masterful job of blinking and quivering, and I was confident that when I tried to talk the nervous stammer would come automatically.

"Kate?" Thad said. "You have such a faraway look in your eyes."

What with all the blinking I was doing, I didn't know how he could tell, but if I did have a faraway look, it was no wonder. I was all the way over in Sunset Landing, ready to shed my mink coat, my upper-class snobbery, and my inhibitions.

"Are you thinking about Rob?"

Rob was so far from my thoughts that I actually blurted out, "Who's Rob?"

I was really embarrassed, but Thad smiled with satisfaction. He must have thought I'd said it deliberately.

"That was my question," he reminded me.

Our miso soup had come. There were no spoons. I picked up my little bowl, copying Thad, and sipped at it. It was very good; I was surprised, because Thad had said it was bean soup and I didn't expect it to be so light and clear.

"He's a friend of mine," I said. At least, he used to be.

"Is that all you're going to tell me about him?"

"That's all there is to tell."

Thad smiled widely. "That's all I wanted to hear."

I put down my bowl because my hands were shaking so hard I was creating tidal waves in my soup. Suddenly my senses all seemed heightened and I was sharply aware of everything around me.

The bright lights were brighter and Thad's face almost seemed to shimmer. The waitresses with their gleaming black hair and bright kimonos looked like exclamation points beside the low tables, and the pungent aroma of exotic foods was accompanied by the hiss and crackle from the open cooking fire.

And swirling out of the speakers above us was the love theme from Tchaikowsky's *Romeo and Juliet*. Of course, it was a souped-up canned-music rendition, but even with the swishy disco beat, it was unmistakably *Romeo and Juliet*.

This was too fantastic to be real.

But it was too real to be a fantasy.

The waitress brought our dinners. Thad's sashimi was a delicately arranged platter of fresh fish, in various shapes and colors. When he asked if I wanted to taste a piece of tuna, I didn't even hesitate. I forgot any qualms I'd had about raw fish. It was delicious.

"Do you like the negima?" he asked.

"It's wonderful. I love it." It was paper-thin slices of steak wrapped around chopped scallions like little brown and green pinwheels.

"I wonder if I could make it," I said between bites. "It doesn't look like it would be too hard."

"Are you a good cook?" Thad asked.

Is this a proposal? Do you have a cast-iron stomach?

"Well . . ." I hesitated. Did it matter if I wasn't the world's greatest cook? Why should Thad care? We'd have a maid and a microwave and the world is full of Japanese restaurants.

"To tell you the truth," I said, "every time I try to cook something interesting and unusual my father says I'm trying to poison him."

"I guess they don't ask you to cook too often." He grinned. He didn't propose, but obviously he didn't care about my culinary deficiencies either.

"And what do you do," he went on smoothly, "when you're not trying to poison your family?"

It was as easy as that. I told him about my friends, my family, about how Beethoven's Violin Concerto made me feel. I told him about my plans for law school, and how I pictured myself arguing for my poor but innocent client with passionate conviction, and persuading a hostile jury that all that damning evidence was purely circumstantial. As I described it to Thad, it was all so vivid again that I got excited just talking about it.

Simply because I got married to Thad, there was no reason to forget about law school and my career. I'd just postpone them for twenty years or so, till the honeymoon was over.

"I like trial scenes too," Thad said.

By now the food was all eaten. The green tea was all drunk. By now Thad knew a whole lot about me—and I still didn't know a thing about him, except that he liked raw fish and had an American Express card. And—somehow—the power to induce heightened sensory perceptions without plying me with mind-altering drugs.

He's the drug, I thought, as we walked through the parking lot. I wondered if the FDA oughtn't require him to carry a warning label.

"It's still pretty early," Thad said. We got into the car. "Why don't you come to my house? I've got a lot of movies on tape. We could have our own double feature."

Aren't we in one? Aren't we making up this movie as we go along? I could see the script outline:

81

Adonis Meets Attorney
Meet cute.
Bump heads.
See stars.
Hear bells.
Lifetime of ecstasy.
The end.

I could hear the studio execs screaming, "It'll never play in Peoria! Who's going to believe it?"

Maybe he wanted me to meet his mother. Thad started the Jag.

Meet his mother. As in: "Mother, I want you to meet the girl I'm going to marry. You two get acquainted and I'll go phone the airport."

The studio execs were right.

Nobody's going to believe this movie.

The big white house was nearly dark as we drove up. It was at the end of a private road, and the only illumination came from the car's headlights. It was a little eerie—not just eerie, but suspicious. For a moment I couldn't help wondering if Thad really had a mother, or if he lived here alone and was planning to surprise me with a private screening of *Sinderella* and *Lust Never Sleeps.*

"Are you sure your mother's home?" I asked nervously. "The house is so dark."

"She's home," Thad said, his voice expressionless. "She doesn't need a lot of light."

What did he mean by that? Maybe his mother was blind and didn't know when it got dark? Or maybe it was just a lame excuse and there actually would be no one in the house but us.

But as soon as Thad opened the front door of his house, I heard the blare of a TV set.

He flipped a light switch and slammed the door behind us. We were standing in a large entry hall. There was a table with a mirror over it on one wall and a closet opposite the mirror. Thad helped me off with my coat and I took a quick look at myself.

I could see Thad in the mirror as he hung up my coat. He closed the closet door and turned around and for a fleeting instant I saw Brick Preston's face reflected behind mine.

I mean, the *real* Brick Preston, the one I saw on TV. It was the cast of the eyes, the set of his mouth, the dark, closed look of repressed anger. In the short time I'd known Thad I'd never seen him truly turn into Brick. I mean, even though Brick and Thad were the same person, Thad didn't seem anything like the role he played. He'd even said so himself.

Maybe once or twice he'd frowned like Brick frowned, but this was different. This was a transformation, as if underneath the surface Thad really was Brick. As if he kept Brick hidden, except during *Lonely Days*. As if, once in a while, in an unguarded moment, like this one, Thad's real personality broke through to the surface.

It seemed bizarre, but there it was. For a few seconds, when Thad didn't realize I could see him, when he wasn't sitting opposite me in a brightly lit restaurant, he'd let his defenses down and stopped acting. The truth, strange as it seemed, was that Thad

83

didn't *act* the part of Brick when he was on TV—he really *was* Brick. "Thad" was an act—the role he played in the "real" world.

I was convinced I was right, because immediately after I caught the glimpse of Brick in the mirror, Thad must have realized I could see him and he instantly transformed his face back into Thad. The eyebrows relaxed, the eyes cleared, the stony look vanished. His mouth was no longer rigid but formed a pleasant, innocuous expression.

I felt as if I'd had the wind knocked out of me. Now I knew what Thad Marshall was really like: Brick Preston. Just the way I'd always imagined him.

"Come on upstairs," Thad said. "We'll go pick out our double feature."

"Upstairs?"

"Sure. The VCR's in my room. Come on."

Maybe I was a more skeptical person than I realized, or maybe it was just my keen legal mind forgetting I was hopelessly in love, but I hesitated. "Did you—uh—leave the TV on when you went out?" I asked.

"What? Oh, no, that's the maid's television."

"Oh, the *maid*. That's who's here." I must have sounded as relieved as I felt, because Thad looked puzzled over my enthusiasm at learning there was a maid in the house watching TV.

"My mother's home too. She wasn't feeling too well when I left. I guess she went to bed early." He looked a little uncertain—as if he couldn't understand the reason he was explaining this.

I couldn't understand myself. Why should I want anyone else around when the only person in the world

84

who mattered to me was about to tell me that I was the only person in the world who mattered to him?

There was no reason for my nervousness. I was being ridiculous and supersuspicious and overimaginative. Even though we were madly in love, Thad seemed to be a perfect gentleman.

But I knew Brick wasn't.

Ten

BRICK'S ROOM WAS something out of a magazine. Not at all like his semisleazy apartment in Sunset Landing. I walked into it, wishing he hadn't hung up my coat downstairs. I wanted to slip it off my shoulders and watch it fall in a heap on the plush gray carpet.

It was more like a study than a bedroom. There was a desk with a leather chair and bookcases behind it. Another wall of shelves held a big TV with a video recorder beneath it, and huge, soft-looking floor pillows in front of it. It seemed to be my night for floors. The bed, a sort of armless sofa with a fitted gray bedsack, was on the other side of the room.

Next to the TV was a sound system. More shelves held audio and video tapes and albums. I wondered what kind of music he listened to. You can tell a lot about a person by the records he owns.

"I can't believe you only just moved in," I said. "How'd you get this place fixed up so fast?"

"We're only renting it," he said. "It came this way.

Most of our own stuff is in the city. We have an apartment there."

"Oh, that explains it. This is such a great room."

"Glad you like it. What are you in the mood for?"

"What?" I'm in the mood for love, but he wasn't supposed to ask a question like that—and here I go thinking in song lyrics again.

"I meant what kind of movie do you want to see?" He flashed a sheepish little grin but I thought I detected a teasing note in his voice, as if he knew just what I'd been thinking.

But he does, I reminded myself. Why do I keep forgetting that? He was used to it; used to women who were helpless in his spell, used to the nervous blinks and quivering lips of beautiful, neurotic females who were too weak to resist his sinister charm.

"I like mysteries," I said faintly, "old ones . . . historical dramas . . . almost anything except Westerns."

He picked through his collection of tapes. "Since you're going to be a lawyer—what a double bill! *Anatomy of a Murder* and *Witness for the Prosecution.* Well, they're both pretty long—"

"Let's watch *Witness for the Prosecution,"* I said. "I love Charles Laughton and I never remember how it ends."

"Me neither."

More proof, I thought with satisfaction, that we were meant for each other. We both loved Charles Laughton and neither of us could remember the end of *Witness for the Prosecution.* Lasting relationships have been built on flimsier foundations than that.

87

He closed the door so we wouldn't disturb his mother, and set up the tape. He arranged some pillows on the floor in front of the TV. After tonight my coccyx would never be the same. I settled down as comfortably as I could in my narrow skirt.

He sat down on the floor next to me, and for about an hour we watched the movie intently. At least, I tried to look intent. I do admire Charles Laughton's performance, but I kept wondering about the performance Thad was putting on. Every once in a while we exchanged comments on the action or made snide remarks about Marlene Dietrich's singing.

There was no sign of the Brick I had glimpsed in the mirror, the Brick who would never bring a woman to his room merely to watch a movie.

Then, just as Dietrich was about to take the witness stand, a woman in aqua hostess pajamas glided into the room.

"I thought I heard you come in, Teddy."

Teddy? Who in the world was Teddy?

He jabbed a button on the remote switch and the picture froze. For a strange moment he seemed to freeze too.

"Aren't you going to introduce me to your little friend?" The woman's voice was hoarse. She sounded almost hurt, as if we were having a party and hadn't invited her.

"This is Kate Bennett. Katie, this is my mother."

We both got to our feet. I took a little longer, because my legs were stiff from an entire evening of sitting funny.

So his mother really was home! He had been telling

the truth; there was no plot to lure me to a dark, empty house and tempt me with old movies.

"Kate Bennett. What a nice, sensible name."

I wasn't sure I liked the sound of that, any more than I liked to be called Brick's (Thad's? *Teddy's??*) "little friend." I wasn't feeling very sensible lately, and I definitely didn't want to be her son's "little friend."

But I remembered my manners.

"How do you do, Mrs. Marshall."

"Pratt, dear. Mrs. Pratt."

Pratt?

"I have to take Katie home now, Mom." He switched off the TV. I glanced at the digital clock on the VCR. It was only 10:30. And we hadn't even seen the end of *Witness for the Prosecution*.

"Must you go so soon?" Mrs. Pratt sounded disappointed. But not half as disappointed as I was. No, I wanted to say, we do *not* have to leave so soon—only it was pretty obvious that for some reason, Brick, Thad, or Teddy was anxious to get out of there.

"I promised Katie's father I'd have her home by midnight."

That just wasn't true. My father had jokingly said, "We like to have her home for Christmas," when Thad asked if I had a curfew, and my mother had said I should use my own judgment. In my judgment, 10:30 was early.

"What a shame. I thought maybe we could sit and chat for a while." That sounded like a good idea, even though it wasn't exactly what I'd pictured. But getting acquainted with my future mother-in-law couldn't hurt. She seemed nice enough, though her voice was a little fuzzy and vague.

"Oh, well," she sighed. "Maybe next time."

Before I could respond, before I could even utter a hasty "Good-bye, nice meeting you," we were hurtling down the stairs and out the door. We barely stopped to grab my coat. I was still trying to zip it as we got into the car.

"Stupid," muttered Thad. "I should have known better."

The Jag zoomed down the dark, narrow lane as if it were driven by a madman. I held my breath until we reached the main road, where we had to stop and wait to turn.

What in the world had gone on back there? What was stupid? What should Thad have known better? And why did his mother call him Teddy and why was her name "Mrs. Pratt," and why had Thad dragged me out of there so fast?

And how did *Witness for the Prosecution* end?

"I was kind of surprised when your mother called you Teddy," I said tentatively.

"That's my name. My real name. Thaddeus Pratt."

Thaddeus. Thaddeus Pratt. Ted Pratt. It just didn't have the same ring to it as Thad Marshall, let alone Brick Preston. I know it sounds silly, but I was sort of—I don't know—let down, I guess, by the ordinariness of "Ted Pratt."

It conjured up such a different image of him—even though the real Ted (or Thad or Brick) was only inches away from me in the little Jaguar.

For instance, I had imagined us having breakfast next to the pool in our Hollywood Hills estate. I am in a satin peignoir, he in a silk robe. I imagined saying, lazily, "Pass me a croissant, will you, Thad darling?"

I could not imagine saying, "Pass the bread, Ted."

Or: I am taking a luxurious bubble bath in the black marble tub before a major studio premiere. The ivory and gold phone next to the bathtub rings. I pick it up (I merely have to dangle my hand over the edge of the tub to reach it) and Dylan's shrill singsong nearly pierces my eardrum. "Kate Pratt, got too fat, sat on a cat, and it went splat. Nyahh."

Kate Pratt. It sounded terrible. Especially when Dylan nyahh-nyahhed it that way. Of course, I could keep my own name. Lots of women are doing that these days, especially professional women—as I would be. Eventually. When the pool began to pall and I got tired of luxury, bubble baths, and ecstasy.

What a difference a name makes, I mused. A rose by any other name *wouldn't* smell as sweet; otherwise why did Cary Grant change his name from Archibald Leach? How come John Wayne couldn't carry bayonets and six-shooters and otherwise typify machoness before he ditched his real name—Marion Morrison?

"Well, here we are."

I looked up, startled. We were parked in my driveway. Already? So soon? This is it? Date's over? Lifetime of ecstasy postponed? Or permanently canceled? On account of *what*?

Should I just get out of the car, walk into the house, and close the door behind me without a backward glance at what might have been? Thad had not turned off the engine.

"Katie, I'm sorry about tonight."

I turned to look at him. His head was lowered, eyes fixed on his knees.

"But I had a marvelous time," I said. "I loved the Japanese restaurant and—"

"And what? Meeting my mother? Look, my mother isn't well. I mean, she seemed okay before I left, so I took a chance, but . . . It was stupid bringing you there."

"She seemed okay to me," I said. "I don't know her or anything, so I guess I can't tell, but I thought she was a perfectly nice person."

"Let's say she's a little . . . unpredictable." He seemed to choose his words carefully, but this didn't help clear up my confusion. Had he been worried that she'd faint, or throw up, or suddenly be seized by a raging fever and become delirious?

That's it! I thought. That must be it. She's mentally ill and just now recovering from a nervous breakdown. And for some reason Thad felt he had to hide that from me; maybe she had an obscure type of hereditary psychosis and Thad might be carrying it in his genes, and he didn't know yet how I felt about having children.

And he must have been afraid she'd say or do something weird, embarrass him in some way; that's why he'd hustled me out of there, to make sure I wouldn't be repelled at the prospect of having a mother-in-law who talks to ashtrays. (Big deal. My father speaks to walls. In unfinished houses. And he claims to be the most well-adjusted person in the world.)

"I understand," I said gently. I wanted him to know it didn't make a bit of difference to me if his mother was a wee bit wacky. We could always adopt.

He turned off the motor. "You know, Katie, it's strange, but I feel like I've known you for a long time. Not at all like we just met this week." His voice was soft and warm.

"But we didn't," I whispered. "I've known you for months." I don't know if he understood what I meant, if he even wanted to understand. He just said, strangely, "No, not *me*," and put his hands on my shoulders and kissed me. First my hair, then right next to my eyebrow. Nobody had ever kissed me next to the eyebrow before. I didn't know what to do, except blink, like Allison, and try to breathe in a quiet, ladylike fashion.

And then I closed my eyes and felt him kiss my cheek, my other cheek, my earlobe, my chin, my lips.

Just as he'd kissed Brooke, just as he'd kissed Allison; I was Brooke, I was Allison. I was swimming in a dreamlit sea and I never wanted to come up for air.

But we finally did. His hands were still on my shoulders as I sighed deeply. "Oh, Brick . . ." His fingers suddenly tightened and then he let go of me.

I leaned back against the seat. For a moment there was silence and then he said, "Kate?"

"Hmm?"

"Who's that leaning out of the window?"

I opened my eyes. "What window?"

"Over there." Thad ducked his head a little and pointed out the passenger side. I looked out and up toward the top floor of our house.

"Actually, it looks more like he's hanging out," Thad said. "Is that Dylan?"

"Oh my God!" It was Dylan, and it did look as if he

were hanging out the window. The top half of him was over the sill and he seemed to be balancing entirely on his stomach.

I jumped out of the car and screamed, "Dylan, you get back inside before you fall out!"

"I'll go in if you give me a quarter."

The light in my parents' bedroom went on.

"And if you give me a dollar for blackmail," Dylan shouted, "I won't tell what you were doing!"

Just then someone yanked him back into the room and slammed the window shut. I sagged against the car, relieved and embarrassed. I fervently hoped that my parents, who don't believe in spanking, were, at this very moment, stringing my little brother up by his thumbs.

Thad was suddenly at my side, standing in the driveway. Now the date *was* over. Dylan had shattered our romantic interlude, axed the ecstasy, blitzed the bliss. The Littlest Hun does it again.

"Cute kid," said Thad. He didn't say it sarcastically.

"Tons of fun," I muttered.

We walked up to the door. I fumbled for my key. "Would you like to come in for a while? We could have some—uh—coffee or something." Preferably "or something."

"I'd better not," he said. "I ought to check on my mother."

He took the key from me and unlocked the door. I was perfectly capable of unlocking my own door, but when he pressed his fingers around mine and kissed the back of my wrist, I was very glad I hadn't insisted on unlocking the door myself. I was also dizzy with the romance and sophistication of being kissed on the wrist, which took my breath away, made my fingers go limp and is probably why I dropped the key.

"Oh, dear . . ."

I urged Thad not to bother looking for it, that it would be easier to find in the daylight, and that this was an extremely low crime area. Besides, I would rather he not waste time on his knees looking for my key when he could be proposing marriage.

We stood for a moment, framed in the light that spilled out through the open door. "Katie?" His voice was tentative. "I'm not used to this, you know. I don't really know what you expect. I mean, if I'm going too fast, or—"

"No, no!" I assured him. "You're doing fine. This is just about right." Actually, I had sort of hoped to have the airline tickets tucked into my jet bag by now, but that may have been a little unrealistic.

I hesitated at the door, reluctant to let him go, reluctant to let go of the whole evening. "You're sure you don't want to come in?"

"I want to very much," he said. "But I can't."

He hugged me hard. I pressed my cheek against his sweater, hugging back.

"Goodnight, Katie."

Eleven

I DIDN'T SEE much of Thad the following week. He drove me to school in the morning but had to stay every afternoon for extra help or tutoring.

Now that he was coming to his classes at the same time everyone else did, a lot of the hoopla seemed to die down. The kids were getting used to seeing him in the halls and in the classroom and they began to take his presence almost for granted.

Thad told me the principal had thought that familiarity would be more effective than isolation in helping the students adjust to Thad, and Thad to the school.

It seemed to be working. Except for a stream of questions about Brick's death, and demands to know who done it, the students began to treat him almost as casually as anyone else.

I, on the other hand, had suddenly achieved minor celebrity status.

Now that they weren't treating Thad like a star, they were treating me like a starlet, just because I was the person closest to him. I thought it was ironic that people seemed to be able to handle Thad's stardom—but couldn't get used to my connection to it.

Maybe because they couldn't believe it. Just like I hadn't at first. But as the week went on, and Thad kept picking me up every morning and standing with me in the hall before Math every afternoon, I had to accept that he did like me. A lot. Maybe he didn't realize yet that I was to be his grand passion, that he was destined to spend the rest of his life with me on the Ecstasy Express, but I hadn't imagined Saturday night, and Thad's car in our driveway every morning was no mirage.

On Tuesday he asked me to save the whole weekend for him: Friday and Saturday nights. We didn't make any definite plans about what to do, but that didn't matter. As long as we were together, the details weren't important.

I kind of enjoyed my new image at school. It was really odd that simply because Thad was interested in me I suddenly became interesting to everyone else. I guess that since they couldn't figure out what my hidden allure was—after all, I'd kept it pretty well hidden up till now—they were intrigued. They didn't understand what Thad saw in me.

You couldn't blame them. I wasn't sure myself.

It drove people like Kenny Greco crazy. In Math he would look from me to Liza Mansfield and back again, shake his head in bewilderment, and mutter, "That's show biz."

Whenever I saw Rob he nodded to me politely and kept walking. I wished I knew what he was thinking. I wondered if he were as hurt as he seemed to be on Friday afternoon, or maybe even more hurt, now that he knew what was going on. Did he think I'd made a fool of him, or betrayed him? Did he hate me? Or did he really not care that much?

Maybe he hadn't had strong feelings for me any more than I'd had for him. Maybe he'd kissed me all those times out of a sense of duty. Maybe he'd felt it was expected of him because we were "going" together. All the while he may have been as blasé about our tepid relationship as I was.

That was sort of a relief; at least I didn't feel so guilty when I could persuade myself that Rob wasn't suffering.

Friday night Thad took me to see a movie. It was a Brazilian film, and there weren't many people in the small theater. If any of them recognized Thad, they didn't bother us.

But when we came out of the theater, something really funny happened. A middle-aged woman in a fur coat and diamonds strolled past us, leading a chihuahua on a leash. She was talking to him in a bright, encouraging voice as she led him along the curb. Suddenly, she turned around, did a double-take, and marched back to where we were standing.

When she was barely a foot away, she peered up at Thad and said, in an incredulous voice, "But you're *dead*. I saw it with my own eyes."

"Not really," Thad said gently. "It's only a television show."

"You mean you're not really dead? Does Allison know? Have you told her? And poor Brooke—I'm going to write to her right now. Someone ought to tell the authorities! Come on, Pepe."

The woman hurried off, yanking Pepe along behind her.

I began to laugh. "Is she kidding? Does she really think—"

"She's not kidding," Thad said. "You'd be surprised how many people think the show is real. Most of our letters come addressed to our characters, not to us. You should see some of my mail."

"I can't believe people are so dumb. Don't they know they're watching television?"

"I don't know. I don't understand it either. But it happens all the time."

"But the show isn't even that realistic," I said. "I mean, it's so far-fetched. And that trial is a joke. . . ."

"You think so? You really think so?" His eyes were so dark, so serious.

"Yes, I really think so." I didn't know what he wanted to hear. I didn't know why it was so important. I just said what I really felt, and hoped it was right. The show *was* far-fetched and not a bit realistic. "Except for you," I added. "You're real. You were always real."

He looked away, and suddenly his eyes seemed hooded, guarded, as if there were emotions he didn't want me to see and secrets he still wanted to keep.

He couldn't be insulted, because what I'd said was a compliment, but something had shifted; I could feel something in the atmosphere between us that hadn't been there before the woman stopped us.

He put his hand on my shoulder and steered me to the parking lot. He didn't so much help me into the car as push me in. He slammed the door and slid into the driver's seat. He had the keys in his hand and he pressed his closed fingers behind my head and kissed

99

me until I was shaking, until I didn't know if what I was feeling was fear or pleasure.

Because now I knew what had changed. He had dropped all pretense of being Thad. He was Brick.

He rammed the key into the ignition and gunned the motor. I sat there, shivering, my hands limp in my lap. He eased up on the accelerator and the engine idled quietly. I looked at him from the corner of my eye. He was clutching the steering wheel as if he were trying to contain his anger, control his emotions, hold on to *something*.

"Do you really know me, Katie? Do you really want to know me?" His voice was low and I thought it sounded almost menacing. I couldn't answer him. I didn't know what answer he wanted. I didn't know what answer I wanted to give.

This was Brick with the mask off, the genteel disguise peeled away. This was the Brick I had only glimpsed in Thad, but the Brick I had known for so many months and in so many dreams.

When I still didn't reply, he threw the car in gear and roared out of the parking lot. We headed north and I realized we weren't driving toward my house, but to his. When I looked over at him I saw the same look of fierce singlemindedness that Brick had had in his last scene with Brooke, as he drove crazily down the Beach road.

I swallowed hard and huddled against the seat. I thought I knew what he was asking. If it was his real self that I wanted him to show me, if it was Brick that I wanted, then that's what I'd get. And the warning in his voice reminded me of all the things Brick was, the smoldering, brooding passions that could not always be suppressed, the dark, unpredictable moods, the danger.

He'd meant me to be frightened. He wanted me to see the choice I had to make, between accepting him as he really was, or being safe with a Thad who presented no threats, no risks, no rough edges.

We turned onto the private drive that led to his house. Halfway up the road he swung the car over to the side, onto the grass under a clump of trees. He cut the motor, turned off the headlights. It was black. There was no moon and the trees that loomed over us blocked out the stars.

He took hold of my shoulders, and kissed me, very hard, very briefly.

"Is this the way you want it, Katie?" His voice was strained, angry. I tried to answer, but I couldn't, I could only feel and hear—the sting his lips left on mine and an almost terrible roaring in my ears. I wondered if this was how it felt when you were about to faint, in the moment before everything went dark.

He let me go so suddenly that I fell back against the door. I heard our ragged breathing, the only sounds in the dark, closed car, and somehow this was frightening too.

I couldn't see his face, only the outlines of him. He pulled at my arm and I thought he was going to kiss me again.

"Brick," I whispered helplessly, and the name seemed to hang in the air like your breath on a cold winter morning. But he only pulled me away from the door so I could lean back against the seat.

"Okay," he said grimly. "Now I know." He started the car and pulled back onto the road that led to his house.

He was right. Because now I knew too. I wanted Brick. I'd had tameness, normality, safety, and been bored with it. Wasn't that just my complaint about Rob? The usually bland, matter-of-fact kisses, the absence of strong feeling, the lack of bells?

It was the very oppositeness of Brick Preston that had attracted me, from the first moment I had seen his troubled face, his piercing eyes, his dark presence glowering at me from Amy's television screen.

All the time I had spent with Thad I'd waited for the momentary flashes of Brick. Now he was admitting that I'd been right, that "Thad" was a personality he put on in polite company, that Brick was who he really was, and who he would be for me, if I were brave enough and honest enough to deal with reality.

I didn't feel brave. As he drove up to the house and screeched to a stop in front of the garage, I was almost terrified. I didn't know what would happen next, I didn't know what he was thinking, I didn't know what I might be getting myself into.

I only knew that like every other woman I was helpless in his spell. I could only remind myself that no one ever said grand passion wasn't scary.

Twelve

THIS TIME THERE was no polite ceremony of helping me off with my coat, hanging it in the closet. Brick simply led me through the entry hall, past the living room to a room with double mahogany doors. He opened the doors and motioned for me to go in. Slowly, deliberately, he pulled the doors shut behind us. I heard a solid metallic click as they locked together.

We were in a library with dark paneling, leather couches, oriental rugs. At any other time I would have stood there, admiring it, exclaiming over it, running my fingers over the soft leather, the leaded windowpanes, wishing I had a room like this. There was even a window seat, where you could curl up on a soft, rainy day and listen to Chopin while you drowsed over a volume of poetry.

But now there was blackness outside the diamond windowpanes and brass lamps provided only small pools of light, so that much of the room was dim and filled with shadows.

Brick took off his jacket and threw it over a chair. I

made no move to undo my coat; not only because I wasn't sure my fingers could work the toggles and the zipper. Maybe if I kept my coat on I wasn't making any commitment, I wasn't admitting anything to Brick.

"Is your mother home?" I asked nervously.

"Does it make any difference?"

I realized it didn't. Even if she were there, she was probably far away upstairs, in her own room, in her own world.

He walked slowly toward me. Instinctively I took a step backward. I bumped against a couch and froze, not knowing which way to move, not able to look away from his eyes even long enough to find somewhere to run.

"Are you afraid of me?" He reached for the belt of my coat and untied it. He began to undo the toggles, quickly, efficiently, his fingers having no trouble with them. I was shaking and I knew he could see it. I was on the verge of tears when he slid the zipper of my coat open in one swift, decisive motion. The metal hiss was a shock in the silent room. I felt it in my spine, like chalk on a blackboard.

He dropped my coat on the couch. I felt cold without it.

"No pretense, right, Katie? No more phoney little dating games. And no more polite chatter, right, baby? 'How does it feel to make love in front of the camera, what college are you going to, how's your mother feeling today?' None of that. I know what you think you want. Better than you do."

Oh, God, I was so cold.

His voice was bitter. I still couldn't understand why

he seemed so angry. Maybe it was because I had seen
through his facade and discovered a personality that
frightened him as much as it frightened me.

He moved away from me and started to prowl the
room restlessly. I'd seen him do this so many times on
Lonely Days.

"My mother said to me once, 'Be careful what you
wish for, because you'll probably get it.' Think about
that sometime. You want to know about my mother?
You want to know where she is? It's truth time, isn't
it?" He stopped pacing. He leaned against a bookcase,
his arms folded in front of his chest.

"Sit down, Kate. And stop looking like a scared
rabbit. I don't like it . . . whatever you might think."

I sat down. I didn't know what to think. I was still
cold, but I wasn't shaking anymore.

"My mother's a drunk. That's her sickness. Right
now she's in a hospital in the city, drying out."

"Oh, I'm sorry!"

Brick moved over to a window and looked out into
the darkness. His back was to me and I studied his firm,
straight shoulders. I imagined I could see the rigid line
of his spine right through his blue sweater.

"My father sent us to live in New York when I was
seven. He's with the State Department. He said travel-
ing around all the time was no life for a kid. What he
really meant was we cramped his style. He had a lot
of . . . 'international *alliances.*' Still does.

"They're not divorced. We see him once in a while.
He's all she ever wanted, since she was twenty. Well,
she got him. Sometimes she can convince herself she
still has him."

105

I wanted to go over to him, to rest my cheek on his shoulder, to touch his back and feel the tension flow out of him.

I probably should have. But I didn't. I thought how hard this must be for him, if he can't even look at me. And if he wanted to be touched, he wouldn't be standing half a room away, keeping himself in the shadows and staring out a window at nothing.

"Life is all accidents," he said abruptly. He turned away from the window and started pacing again. "And you never can tell what's going to happen to you, because everything that happens is a fluke. You know how I became an actor? By accident. A director spotted me in Foodtown when I was ten years old. You know how I got the part on *Lonely Days?* The head writer had insomnia one night and saw me in a TV commercial at four-thirty in the morning. And how did you and I end up here? We accidentally knocked our heads together in a room we both happened to be in."

"But aren't those lucky accidents?" I said finally. My voice was soft, but he heard me. "I'm very glad we bumped heads."

"That's not the point. The point is you can't control it, and you can't predict it and you can't plan for it." He moved to the front of the couch and stood over me, so I had to look up at him. "No matter how hard you try," he said.

He sounded so bitter, so alienated . . . so much like Brick Preston. Maybe it wasn't surprising. After all, Brick's father had deserted *him* too.

"What about fate?" I asked. "Or destiny. Maybe we were destined to meet. And if we hadn't met now, we would have met a year from now—somewhere. I mean, how likely is it that we'd ever meet at all, Brick. You're an actor and I'm just—"

"My name is Thad. Not Brick. Stop calling me that."

I looked away, embarrassed. "I'm sorry. I just forgot. I'm so used to—I mean, the way you're acting—"

"I'm acting just the way you expected, Katie. Just the way you imagined. Isn't that true?"

There was that question again, raw and unvarnished, demanding a straight yes or no answer, just like in a courtroom, where the truth had to be raw and unvarnished, not softened with any elaborations or excuses.

I thought of his mother, about being careful what you wished for. I thought of how long I'd wished for him, how much I loved him, how I'd dreamed of a moment like this, so I could tell him how I felt, and hear him tell me.

It was truth time.

I got up, feeling clear-eyed and clearheaded. I wasn't trembling and I knew I didn't feel like a scared rabbit any more.

"Yes," I said. "You *are* what I wished for. You're exactly what I wished for, exactly the way you are. You said no pretending, no games, and you've been asking me all night to tell you how I really feel. Maybe I was afraid to before, but I'm not now."

"Katie." His voice was a warning, but strangely, now *he* took a step back away from me. Was he afraid to hear the truth, frightened by what *he* was seeing in *me?*

"Truth time," I repeated. "That's what you said. I'm sorry about your mother, I really am, but whatever she said, I'm a very logical person and I know what I want, and you're right to tell me to be honest about it. I wished for you."

I stopped myself and took a deep breath.

"I can't believe I'm saying this. You don't know how hard this is—telling you first, and not knowing how *you* feel, I mean, *really* feel about me—and just—hoping you won't laugh."

The strangest look flashed across his face, like pain, or disappointment, or something else I couldn't figure out. For a moment I was cold again, and felt sure that he was about to say something that would break my heart.

"I'm not laughing," he said. "Believe me, I'm not laughing."

Only then did I realize I'd been holding my breath. I let it out with a little sigh. He reached for me. Everything seemed to be in slow motion as he pulled me into his arms and kissed me. For a moment he held me so tightly I couldn't breathe, and then he released his grip.

"I'd better take you home now."

I certainly hadn't expected *that*.

"Say something to me," I whispered. "I told you, you made me tell you, and now you won't tell me."

"I thought I just did," he said quietly. He got my coat and put it around me. I could hardly push my arms through the sleeves. He zipped it up, then carefully fastened each closing, as if he were dressing a child. His eyes never left my face.

He tied my belt tightly around my waist. "You're not careful enough what you wish for, Katie."

108

"Can't you just say you love me?" I hated myself for saying it, but I couldn't help it. "Is it that hard?"

"It's easy." He leaned his shoulder against the door, one hand on a brass knob. "I do love you. *You*, Kate, just the way you were the day you dropped all your books." His voice sounded soft, gentle, a little wistful. I was so happy, so relieved, that I nearly did start to cry then. My eyes were blurry as he closed the double doors behind us.

When we got to my house, he didn't even turn off the Jag's engine. He just shifted into neutral and set the brake. He reached over and grasped the end of my coat collar, pulling until our lips met in a quick kiss. He let me go and took a deep breath—as if he needed to collect himself, to prepare himself to talk.

"I'll pick you up at eight-thirty tomorrow. We're going to a party." His voice wasn't soft and gentle anymore. "In the city. Might as well have all your dreams come true."

"What do you mean?" I was still breathless from his kiss, and drunk with knowing that he loved me. The only dream I had left was that he would kiss me again. Right now.

"A lot of people from the show will be there. You'll get to see Dr. Paul's real hair. And Morgan Fontayne and Alana Bainbridge—God, all the women I've seduced and abandoned."

"Really?" I nearly shrieked. "I can't believe it!"

I sounded like a dippy fan, I knew I did. I wasn't star-struck or anything, I never had been, but to see what all those actors were really like, to meet Brooke

109

and Nicole and Allison in *person,* after seeing them all these months on television—who wouldn't be at least a *little* thrilled at the thought of a night of tinsel and glitter?

"Brick, this is so exciting!" I was gushing.

"My devastating charm often has that effect on people," he said sarcastically. "And my name is Thad."

"What should I wear?"

"Who the hell cares what you wear?"

"Thad! What a terrible thing to say."

"I mean, wear whatever you want. I mean, I don't give a damn what you wear, because you look adorable even in that idiotic overstuffed coat, and nobody else will give a damn what you wear because they'll be so involved with how *they* look."

He leaned past me and opened the door. "Katie, go inside. It's been a long night and I'm tired. I'll see you tomorrow."

I slid out of the car, still hearing how he'd said I looked adorable to him even though he hated my coat. I don't think anyone, not even my parents, had thought I was adorable since I was two years old.

I looked at my watch. "It's only eleven-thirty," I said. "It hasn't been such a long night."

"Count your blessings."

He slammed the passenger door shut and I stood there, dumbly, in the driveway, wondering why he wasn't walking me to the door. He rolled his window down and said, "Get in the house! I want to see you go inside."

Obediently I walked up the front steps, groping inside my bag for the key. I opened the door and let myself in. I heard him rev the motor a few times before he drove away.

I was such a jangle of emotions, I didn't know what I felt or what to think. I walked slowly upstairs wondering, absurdly, what to wonder about first.

The whole evening had been like a dream, *another* dream. Even if I didn't agree with Thad about everything being an accident, maybe he was right about not being able to control or predict what would happen to you, any more than you can control a nightmare once it begins to disturb your sleep.

I'd gotten what I'd wished for, but from what I had seen of Thad tonight, and what I'd already known about Brick, I realized that from here on, events were out of my hands.

Maybe I wouldn't complain about my bland, ordinary life anymore, that was the only thing I could be sure of. I might as well have been Brooke or Allison or Nicole; I was an actress in my own fantasy.

But I was no longer writing the script.

Thirteen

"Mom, you know your white jumpsuit?"

"The satin one that I got on sale at Filene's that was so expensive I couldn't afford it even on sale? The one that still has the price tag on it because I haven't worked up the nerve to wear anything that glamorous yet?"

"Yeah, that's the one."

"Kate, that was for *me* to wear someplace *soigné* and sophisticated. *I haven't even taken the price tag off.*"

"Mother, please, you haven't needed something sophisticated and *soigné,* whatever that is. That's why the price tag is still on it. I have *got* to have your jumpsuit tonight. This is a *show business* party. I can't wear a pleated skirt."

"Kate, I'd cut off my right arm for you—"

"I don't need your right arm, I need your jumpsuit!"

"Take it," she said, defeated. "Go, get stardust on it. It would enjoy that. I'm going into the office to sulk."

"Thank you!" I threw my arms around her. "I love you!"

"I love you too, but I'm still going to sulk."

I called Amy, who, as I'd expected, went absolutely crazy at the news of the party. Even more crazy than at the news that Thad really loved me. I didn't go into too many details about that, because there were too many details I didn't understand myself.

"Katie, sneak me in the trunk! Take notes! Take a camera! Take a tape recorder!"

I called Stephanie. "Steph, it's the Real Thing, and I don't know whether I'm scared or thrilled or *what*. Do you realize I don't even know how *old* he is? Listen, you work with all those records, maybe you—"

"Nineteen," she said.

"Nineteen? Why didn't you tell me? You knew all along?"

"You didn't ask me," she said. "Besides, it's confidential. Why didn't you ask him?"

"I never got the chance. Nineteen? He seems older. Much older . . ."

"That's show biz."

"Steph, this is serious. We spent the whole night talking."

"Really?" There was distinct interest in Stephanie's voice. And the merest hint of a leer. "The whole night? Talking?"

"Don't be crude," I said coolly. "This is much more complex than you think. I can't even begin to tell you."

"When you're ready to begin," she said, "I'm all ears."

It was complex. And it was mystifying. And I'd spent an extremely restless night. I woke up, determined not to care, not to worry. You have to go with the experience, I thought, to accept love. You have to let someone else write the script sometimes.

I tried on my mother's jumpsuit. It was dazzling. I don't think I ever would have worked up the nerve to wear anything so arrestingly glamorous, so aggressively attention-getting, so *satin* until today.

I took a bath in Reckless Abandon. I listened to *Romeo and Juliet*. I listened to Rachmaninoff's Second Piano Concerto. I listened to Ravel's "Bolero."

I sat in the den and contemplated Attila. The Littlest Hun was only seven, but a potential man. Some day, if he grew up, he would fall in love. Someone might even fall in love with him. It was possible that there would be a girl in whom he inspired grand passion. I watched calmly as he nuked Los Angeles on the Atari.

I felt sorry for that girl. A grownup Dylan could be even more dangerous than Brick.

I did my hair and makeup. I filched a pair of ivory and silver combs from my mother's dresser and stuck them in my hair, so they pulled strands up and back on either side of my head. I borrowed my mother's silver shoes. My foot is half a size larger than hers, but that didn't matter.

I knew I wouldn't take my down coat, even if I'd been so gauche as to think it was suitable to wear over white satin. My mother had an embroidered mandarin jacket. It was quilted and wasn't really meant to be worn as a coat, and certainly not in February, but that's what I'd wear.

Silver earrings, delicate little chains that dangled and peeked out from my hair whenever I moved my head. Those were my own. This was the first time I was wearing them.

I called down to my parents, "Come and look at me!"

I stood, imperiously, in the middle of my room, not moving until they entered.

"Am I," I asked, turning slowly around so they could get a full view of me, "half as devastating as I think I am?"

"You're twice as devastating as you think you are," my father said. He sounded a little annoyed about it. "What's wrong with what you wore last week?"

"I wore it last week," I said patiently.

"My combs," my mother muttered. "My shoes. My jumpsuit."

"And your mandarin jacket," I said.

"Of course. Naturally. But you'll be cold."

"No I won't."

"Lenore," my father said, "she's going to a party in the city. With actors. *Producers.*"

"She'll probably come back with a contract."

I glowed quietly.

My father gave her one of his rare, steely glares. "With people much older than she is."

"I won't be alone. Thad'll be with me."

"He is one of them," my father said.

"He's only nineteen," I told him.

"And you're only sixteen."

I glanced at myself in the mirror on the closet door. I couldn't honestly blame my father for worrying. I didn't look sixteen.

"Larry," my mother said, "Kate will be all right. Thad's a nice boy; you know you like him. And she's never done anything to make you worry like this. Let her be beautiful and happy and have a wonderful time."

Beautiful. My mother had said beautiful.

My father just sighed.

"I'll let him in when he comes, all right?" I said anxiously. "Please, would you stay in the den? And keep Dylan tied up?"

My mother grinned. "Sure. And I'll clean all the cinders out of the fireplace while you're at the ball. The mandarin jacket's in my room. The same place you found everything else."

I sat on my wicker chair and waited. Calmly. At least, until 8:25. Then I began to feel the excitement building. I couldn't really stay cool at the prospect of the night ahead.

Thad didn't come at 8:30. By 8:45 I didn't have the least ounce of calm left in me. Where was he? Why didn't he come? Was he standing me up? He was always on time. This wasn't like him.

But it was like Brick.

I was really beginning to panic when the doorbell rang at five to nine. I jumped out of the chair, not even trying to retrieve a semblance of cool. I couldn't run down the stairs in those tight shoes, but if they'd been half a size larger, I would have.

I even forgot how I looked, that my mother said I was beautiful, that my father had said I was devastating. I was so relieved that he was there, so upset that he had made me agonize like this, that I yanked the door open and blurted out, "You're late!"

He stood in the doorway and studied me. Very deliberately. Up and down, from my silver combs, to my silver shoes, and back again.

"And *you're* absolutely . . . mouth-watering."

All of my anger drained out of me, along with a good deal of my backbone.

"What are you auditioning for?" he asked mildly.

"What?"

"I only meant that I'll be afraid to leave you alone at that party for a minute."

"You said it didn't matter what I wore. You said no one would care."

"That was before I knew what you were going to wear. Get your coat and let's get out of here."

I went upstairs to get my mother's jacket. When I came down he was waiting right at the bottom of the stairs, watching me move toward him. He was wearing a plain, close-fitting black sweater and black pants. And this time, a black leather jacket.

As I reached the last step, he took my hand and squeezed it hard. "I can't wait till this party is over."

When we closed the front door behind us, he kissed me.

When we were locked inside his car he said, "Did you bring a lipstick with you?"

"Yes." I didn't know what he was getting at. He pressed his mouth against mine till my bones were melting together like a watercolor left in the rain. When he let go of me he said, "You'd better use it."

He didn't kiss me again, not once, all during the drive into the city. Not even when we were held up for ten minutes at the toll plaza approach to the Midtown Tunnel. He didn't talk very much and the things he said were sort of strange. Like, without any introduction or explanation he said, "You surprise me much more than

117

I thought you could." He even sounded surprised as he said it.

When I told him he looked good in black he just smiled. His smile was strange too. Sort of—I don't know, maybe ironic.

I asked him how his mother was.

"Thirsty," he said. I didn't mention his mother again.

As we were driving uptown, I remembered that he had an apartment in the city. The thought was so disturbing that I buried it immediately, and said something just to distract myself.

"You never told me why you were late," I said. I managed to force a note of reproach into my voice. "You didn't even apologize."

We stopped at a red light. "No," he agreed. He pushed a strand of my hair back from my face and flicked my earring so it swung sideways. "Did you really expect me to?"

I stared out the windshield till the light turned green. I reached up to stop my earring from swinging.

"No," I said. "Not really."

"That's why I didn't."

Fourteen

As we walked from the parking garage to Morgan Fontayne's building Thad said he was really sick of the tinsel and glitter—though he didn't say it that way—and that we were going to be surrounded by phonies, climbers, and people on the make. I wondered, if he hated everyone who was going to be there, and everything they represented, why he'd asked me to go at all.

"Don't believe anything you see," he warned, "or anything you hear. It isn't any more real than *Lonely Days*."

It struck me that the way Thad felt about his fellow actors was exactly the way Brick felt about the people of Sunset Landing.

"Sort of a play within a play?" I suggested.

"That's a good way to put it."

But after fifteen minutes in Morgan Fontayne's apartment, I began to think that Thad was putting on the biggest act of all. If he was sick of the tinsel and glitter, if he really didn't like these people, he was doing a masterful job of covering it up.

Everyone seemed delighted to see him. All the women kissed him. And he kissed them all back. I know people in show business kiss all the time—after all, I *have* seen talk shows—but Morgan Fontayne (Allison) and Alana Bainbridge (Nicole) threw themselves into kissing Thad with such enthusiasm that I began to wonder about Thad's off-screen romances.

Within half an hour Thad, who had promised not to leave my side all evening, had been away from my side for fully fifteen minutes.

He'd introduced me to some people, telling them I was a *fan*. A fan, for heaven's sake. Not his love, not his fiancée, not even his close friend—just some little girl from the suburbs here to get some stardust sprinkled on her.

Then he let himself be captured by Julie St. Clair (Brooke), all blonde and slinky and black jersey. She clung to him the way her dress clung to her. I felt as if I'd been stabbed. I told myself not to believe anything I saw, that this was a play within a play, and all the men and women merely players.

I forced myself to look away from them, to focus on the trendy furnishings, the city nightscape glittering from the terrace window, the beautiful people in their beautiful clothes; even the ones in jeans were beautiful.

Go with the experience, I reminded myself. That's all I can do. I might never have this chance again. I searched out the familiar faces: Dr. Paul, Allison's mother, Bill.

Dr. Paul's hair was thin and getting thinner by the minute. I wondered why he didn't wear a rug all the time. Wouldn't a real phoney do that? Doesn't everyone in show business try to look young?

The room was smoky. The laughter sounded like glass shattering around me. I told myself that Thad was just acting—he was acting "Thad" for all these people —and tried not to wonder why he was bothering. I thought it was ironic that by acting the part of Thad he was treating me just like Brick would. Just like—as Amy would put it—he was crumbling up another paper towel.

My stomach had been in a knot since I'd seen him kiss Brooke on the lips, and the tinsel and glitter were rapidly tarnishing. I could have been invisible. Nobody seemed to know I was there. Thad had been right the first time when he said no one would be looking at me. I wouldn't have cared about that, if only *he'd* look at me.

All of a sudden somebody *was* looking at me. With undisguised appreciation. I hadn't felt beautiful for the last half hour.

"You look good enough to eat," he said. I thought that was sort of blatant, but he was obviously a blatant type. He subscribed to the Tom Jones philosophy of fashion. He wore a gold chain around his neck with one of those crooked tooth pendants that are supposed to symbolize something or other—macho, I guess. His hair was so lush and curly that I felt sure it was permed, and that ever since he'd had it done he'd been waiting for someone to run barefoot through it.

I began to perk up. I was not used to being leered at by male starlets. I wasn't used to flirting either, because I'm not the flirting type, but then, I'd never worn white satin before. There's a first time for everything. This might even be fun.

I batted my eyelashes at him. I really did. He loved

it. He leaned against the wall with one upraised elbow. He took a sip of his drink.

"I haven't seen you around before," he said. "I would have remembered."

"I haven't seen you around either."

"You will. Look at that guy over there." He pointed to a plump, balding man in a shiny yellow shirt. "By the time this party is over we're gonna have a deal. . . . I can't really talk about it yet, but think prime time. Think miniseries."

Prime time, I thought agreeably. Miniseries.

He swung himself around so he was facing me and put both hands on the wall behind me, so I was trapped. Only I wasn't really trapped, because I could very easily duck underneath an arm if the need arose.

"You know what?" he said. "Once this deal goes through I can do things for you. I'm gonna have a lot of clout, casting-wise."

Holy cow, maybe I *would* come home with a contract. I nearly giggled. Instead I gazed into his artificially earnest brown eyes and murmured breathily, "My, how exciting . . . careerwise . . ."

He was licking his lips, like the wolf in Little Red Riding Hood, when Thad materialized at his side. "You work fast," he said to me. His voice was pleasant and bantering, but his face wasn't.

"Not as fast as you do," I replied.

"Hey, Thad Marshall," said my starlet.

"Do I know you?"

"Not yet, but I've seen you on the tube. Hey, man, I really admire your work." He dropped his arms, releasing me, and put out his hand to shake Thad's. "John

Lee Forrest. Listen, I didn't mean to step on any toes. I thought she was alone."

I *was* alone. For the last half hour.

"No problem," Thad said. "Come on, Kate, I want you to meet some people."

As he steered me toward a group near the fireplace he said, "I wouldn't have thought he was your type."

"He isn't. I think I was *his* type."

"Anything in skirts is his type."

Thanks a lot. "I'm not wearing a skirt," I pointed out.

"Just watch yourself."

"I thought you were going to be doing that."

Thad led me over to introduce me to Paxton Thayer (Dr. Paul), who kissed my hand and was very charming. He also introduced me to a woman with short, straight blonde hair, in a sapphire dress, whom I didn't recognize.

"Barbara Jo Conway," Thad said. "One of the writers of *Lonely Days*. Kate Bennett. One of your fans."

There he went again. I tried to ignore it.

"Isn't she *darling?*" Barbara Jo exclaimed. "Where did you *find* her?"

"At school."

"Maybe I should go back to school," Paxton Thayer said gallantly.

I felt like a six-year-old being talked about to my mother.

"Do you enjoy the show?" Barbara asked. At last! Someone was speaking to me.

I hesitated. The truth was obviously not an option in

123

this place. Thad put his hand on my shoulder and gave it a squeeze that may have looked affectionate but felt more like a warning.

"Very much," I lied. "I think you're awfully good," I said to Paxton Thayer. He beamed and murmured, "Lovely child." I thought my nose might start to grow longer any moment now.

"I liked it better before you killed off Brick, though."

Thad smiled modestly and shrugged. I knew I'd said the right thing. And I hadn't even had to lie.

"I know, I know," Barbara moaned. "I fought like a tiger for him, but you know Grace. Once she decides something—"

I didn't know Grace. I must have looked puzzled. Thad said, "Grace Mayne Shantz. She's the head writer."

"You should see the mail," Paxton said. "They must have gotten ten thousand letters this week." Thad looked delighted.

The man in the shiny yellow shirt approached us. He had a big, toothy smile and his face was Santa Claus pink.

"Thad Marshall!" he bellowed. "Good to see you, good to see you. And who is this charming young thing?"

"Kate Bennett," Thad said. "Kate, Harry Kingman, the producer."

"Have I seen you in anything, honey?" he asked me. "What have you done?"

"She's a civilian," Thad said.

"Really? You know," he turned to me, "you're absolutely gorgeous. Have you ever tested?"

124

Suddenly I was having a very good time at this party. I *did* feel like Cinderella at the ball. The idea of coming home with a contract began to seem less and less fantastic.

"Harry, she's a kid from Long Island," Thad said. "She's never done anything."

I was furious. Why did he keep putting me down this way? I could answer for myself. I wanted to enjoy all the compliments I was getting, but Thad wouldn't let me.

I didn't look at him. I looked up at Harry the same way I had looked at John Lee Forrest and said sweetly, "And this is the first time Thad's let me stay out this late."

Harry laughed. "Cute, cute. I can see why he wants to keep you locked up. Say, Thad." He turned away from me. "I have something for you that's going to make you the happiest guy ever written out of a show."

"Yeah, Harry? Terrific."

"I've got something in the works right now. . . ."

Think prime time. Think miniseries.

"Marty still your agent? Over at T.I.?"

"Sure."

"I'll call him."

He turned back to me. He cupped my chin in his hand and kissed me loudly on the mouth. "And you, you gorgeous creature—if you ever decide you want to break into the business, you come and see me."

"Thank you, Mr. Kingman." I batted my eyelashes at him. "It was a thrill and an honor to meet you." He ate it up. I probably could have added, "You great big wonderful man, you," without rousing the least suspicion about my sincerity.

"Excuse us a minute," Thad said to Paxton and Barbara, who had been listening silently to all this. "Time for a refill." He dug his fingers into my arm and led me toward the bar.

"Just what the hell do you think you're doing?" He pulled me past the bar and into the hallway.

"Let go! You're hurting me."

He quickly dropped his hand. I rubbed my arm.

"Why are you acting like this?"

"When in Rome . . . What am I supposed to do while you're off in a corner playing kissy-kissy with Julie St. Clair?"

He looked away. "I told you not to believe anything you saw. I told you it was all phoney—all part of the game."

"Can't I play too?"

"You're an amateur here. You don't even know the rules."

"I'm a fast learner."

"You sure are," he said sourly. "Okay, fine. Go play. If you get in trouble, just scream."

He started to walk away.

"Thad! Thad, wait." He turned back. "Are you really worried about me? Or jealous?"

He tilted his head and looked at me thoughtfully. "Both," he said at last. For a moment, he didn't seem like Brick.

I wanted to go after him, to be with him, to stop all this nonsense. I wanted him to concentrate on me, only me. I wanted us to be together. That was all I really ever wanted.

But before I could take a step to follow him, Brooke was at his side again. He draped his arm over her

126

shoulder and stuck another knife into me. She slid her arm behind his back and her fingers slithered like snakes toward his shoulder blades. She looked up at him, laughing, and their heads stayed close together. I thought I would start to cry, right there.

Morgan Fontayne emerged from a door down the hall and smiled brightly. "You're Thad's friend, aren't you? Why are you standing here all alone? Aren't you having a good time?"

"It's a wonderful party," I said miserably. She followed my eyes to where Brooke and Thad were snuggling and said, "Oh, honey, don't pay any attention to that. It doesn't mean anything. It's ancient history."

Then there *had* been something between them. It didn't look like ancient history at all. It looked very much like current events. The hurt must have been written all over my face, because Morgan gave me a quick little hug and said, "Sweetie, it's a party. Everyone's just having fun. It's not serious. Come on, why don't you have some fun too?"

She took my hand and led me back into the smoky room. We walked right past Thad and Brooke to the grand piano, where a tall blond man in a candy-striped shirt was sipping a drink. He wore cowboy boots.

"Steve, this is—Kate, isn't that right?" I nodded. I had to tilt my head back to look up at him. It was definitely worth the effort.

"Isn't he something?" Morgan whispered. "Now you have fun."

"Thank you, Morgan," I said softly. "You're very nice."

"So is Thad, honey. He really is."

Left alone with the blond gorgeous person, I tried halfheartedly to flirt again, to "have fun," but my heart wasn't in it. Steve didn't mind. He flirted with me. And did most of the talking. He had the starring role in an off-off-Broadway play.

"I'd love you to come see it," he said. "I can have them hold a ticket for you at the box office any time."

"That would be great." I hoped I sounded enthusiastic.

"Name the day, sugar."

My eyes wandered and I saw Thad looking at me. He wasn't with Brooke any more, but in a cluster of other people near the buffet. When he caught my eye he turned away.

I met someone who said he was a set designer. He loved my combs. He actually redid my hair, pulling it higher over the crown of my head and putting the combs back in at different angles. Thad was only a few feet away from us and watched the whole process with narrowed eyes.

A middle-aged man in a three-piece suit made me really uncomfortable. He was a little drunk and coming on very strong. I didn't think this one was merely looking for a bit of flirtatious chitchat.

He kept moving closer and closer to me as he spoke, and I kept stepping back to keep at least a few inches of space between us. He was really leaning on me. I said, "Excuse me," a few times and tried to break away, but he stuck to me like glue.

Finally he shoved his mouth practically against my ear and began to whisper sloppily at me.

I recoiled in disgust, and suddenly two firm, protective hands clasped my shoulders.

The man in the three-piece suit scowled.

Behind me I heard Thad say pleasantly, "Would you mind introducing me to your daughter, sir?"

The man actually started to sputter.

I put my arm around Thad's waist and hugged him. "Thank you. I was just going to yell for help."

"Let's get out of here." He spun me around toward the hallway. "I'll get your jacket."

"Okay. But I have to say thank you to Morgan."

"I thanked her for both of us."

He went down the hall and came back with our jackets. He looked critically at me. "The bathroom's over there," he said. "Go fix your hair."

"Don't you like it this way?"

He pulled the combs out of my hair and dropped them in my hand. "I liked it the way it was. Now, go fix it."

In the bathroom I told myself that he was just jealous. He didn't want to be mean or insulting—he was just telling me he didn't want to share me.

Maybe it wasn't very fair—I'd had to share him, and he'd hurt me, and he didn't seem to care about *my* jealousy—but I was glad all those men had flirted with me, and glad Thad didn't like it.

As we walked to the garage where we'd left the car I began to shiver from the cold.

"That jacket isn't warm enough," Thad said. "You should have worn your coat."

"You don't like my coat."

"I don't like to see you freezing, either." He took his jacket off and put it around my shoulders.

"But you'll be cold," I protested.

"I'll live."

129

He didn't say anything else until we were on the Long Island Expressway. He hadn't said a word about wanting to be alone with me and I had no idea what was going through his mind.

The heater was on full so I didn't need his jacket anymore. I couldn't stand the silence in the car. I wanted to talk about the party. I wanted to know about Julie St. Clair. I wanted him to explain why he'd left me to the sharks, how he could possibly do that if he really loved me.

I looked over at him. He seemed to be concentrating only on driving.

"Thad? Morgan told me you used to go with Julie St. Clair. You never told me that."

"It was a long time ago."

I couldn't stop myself. "You said you wouldn't take your eyes off me all evening—"

"I didn't. You seemed to be having a fine time."

"You know the only reason I was talking to those people was because you weren't around. You know I didn't care about anybody at the party except you. And you ignored me."

"I didn't ignore you."

"Oh, come on. You were so wrapped up in—"

"I wasn't 'so wrapped up.' Julie and I are friends, that's all."

I snorted. "Intimate friends."

"Not anymore. You have no reason to be jealous, Kate. I was just doing what was expected of me."

"What *she* expected?"

"What everyone expected. What everyone was doing."

"Then why are you so angry that I did it?"

He exploded. "Because I didn't expect *you* to act that way!" He paused, as if he were trying to control himself. "I didn't like it," he added. His voice was much lower.

"How do you think I felt?"

"I know how you felt. And I know I have no right to be angry. I really didn't want to hurt you."

"But you did."

"I'm sorry. I told you you weren't careful enough about what you wished for."

He drove me straight home. He parked the Jag in the driveway and walked me up the steps to the door.

"Will you come in?" I asked.

He took my face in his hands and kissed me, so sweetly. Not at all like he was angry, not as if he were repressing dark and dangerous impulses, just like he loved me, simply and uncomplicatedly.

"Katie? Am I still what you want?"

"More than ever," I whispered.

"Even after the way I was tonight?"

"*Yes.*" I knew he was sorry he'd hurt me. And whatever else he'd done, he stirred feelings in me I'd never experienced before. Maybe I'd simply never *felt* before. If you loved someone as much as I loved Thad you had to accept the fact that you were vulnerable. You had to face the possibility of being hurt. You had to learn to forgive.

"Oh, Katie." He sighed and pressed his hands against my cheeks. He kissed my hair and traced my ears with his fingers, right down to the posts of my earrings. "I love you like this," he whispered. I didn't know what he meant, except that he loved me.'

"Brick . . . ," I murmured.

He dropped his hands from my face and stuck them in his pockets. "Good night, Katie."

"Aren't you going to come in? Are you still angry about the party?"

"I'm not angry about the party. I'm just—really tired. I'll see you."

I didn't understand. But it was all right, I told myself as I unlocked the door. He'd said he loved me. That was the only thing that mattered. But, just, "I'll see you"?

I closed the door behind me and kicked off the silver shoes. My mother was standing at the top of the stairs. I wasn't surprised that she'd waited up for me.

"Did you have a good time?" she whispered. "Was it wonderful? Was my jumpsuit a success?"

Suddenly I felt exhausted.

"Your jumpsuit got me an audition, a part in a miniseries, a free ticket to an off-off-Broadway show called *Chicken Fetters,* and an indecent proposal. I turned them all down."

"That's my sensible Kate," she said fondly.

I handed her the jacket and shoes and she kissed me good night.

"Of course," she added, "you might want to reconsider the miniseries."

Fifteen

THAD DIDN'T CALL me on Sunday. He hadn't said he would, but I kept waiting for the phone to ring. I told myself that he had a lot of studying to catch up on. But I couldn't help feeling let down.

Stephanie and Amy came over for a while to hear about the party. Amy practically frothed at the mouth as I described it. Even Stephanie was impressed.

They dismissed my doubts about Thad very lightly.

"You're just not used to actors," Amy said. "Or love."

"Simple lack of experience," Stephanie agreed. "You can't expect to understand him, not this soon. He's too far out of your realm. You come from different worlds."

Maybe they were right. But how could I not be confused and disturbed by the way Thad acted toward me? I couldn't stop wondering how he really felt, what he was really thinking when, at any moment, he might shift gears and throw me completely off balance. And I didn't know what he expected of me. I couldn't figure out how he wanted me to act. Because that too seemed to change from one moment to the next.

He loves me, I kept telling myself. That's what counts. If he loves me, everything will be all right.

Thad drove me to school every day that week and never had he seemed more like Brick. In fact, he was the darkest, moodiest Brick Preston I had ever seen. I'd sit next to him in the car, trying timidly to make conversation, to bring him out of his blackness. He'd give me curt, almost rude responses, not seeming to care how I reacted to what he said, not weighing his words for the impact they had on me.

We'd stand outside Mr. Gelber's room before the bell rang. He'd rest his hand lightly on the back of my neck, making me feel like there was an electric current running from his fingertips straight down my spine. But he didn't speak to me. He had a smile and a cheerful greeting for everyone who passed by, but no words for me.

After school we would walk to his car and he would drive me home. He would kiss me—very professionally, very much the way he kissed on camera, and only once.

He didn't come into the house with me. He didn't make any excuses about having to work, he just let me out of the car and drove off; I spent the rest of the afternoon and all night trying not to cry.

By Thursday I was a frazzled, disoriented, nervous wreck. I looked and sounded like Brooke, just before she got amnesia. This was not what I'd imagined; this was no part of my dream. I couldn't stand it anymore.

When we got to my house Thursday afternoon Thad kissed me once, and reached across me to open the car door. I grabbed the handle and slammed the door shut.

"Why are you doing this to me?"

For a second he looked startled. Not angry, just surprised. Then he got that hooded look in his eyes and said mildly, "What are you talking about?"

I wanted to scream. I wanted to hit him. He knew exactly what I was talking about. Why was he pretending not to?

"Are you still angry about the party?" I asked.

"No. I told you I wasn't."

"You told me you loved me, too. Have you—stopped? Did you ever mean it?"

"Yes."

"Yes, *what*? Which one?"

"I told you the truth!" he shouted. "Even though I didn't think you'd believe it."

"How can I? When you treat me like—like a used paper towel?"

"What?"

"Forget it." I closed my eyes tightly, trying to keep the tears in. How could he love me if he didn't care how badly he was hurting me?

"What do you want?" he asked. "Just tell me what you want from me."

"To believe you."

"I can't make you believe me," he said dully.

"Why don't you want to try? You won't talk to me, you don't want to be with me. You push me out of your car every day."

There was a long silence. I twisted my hands in my

lap, waiting for him to tell me something that would make everything all right.

"Can I come in for a while," he asked finally, "and try to convince you?"

He said it so casually, as if it really didn't matter to him one way or another. I felt sick. I tried to sound like I had some pride left but it was hard to act dignified when I was choking back tears. "Not if you don't want to."

"But I *do* want to," he said fervently. "Oh, Katie, I *do*."

When Dylan came home from school he found us in the den. I was so groggy with kisses and happiness that I felt drunk. I wouldn't even let Dylan's pointed remarks get to me.

"How come you don't kiss Rob anymore?"

"Because I like Thad now."

"I like Rob better."

"Then you go kiss him."

Dylan looked Thad straight in the eye and said, "I don't like you."

"That's all right. Sometimes I don't like myself much either."

He said it to Dylan but I knew he was really saying it to me. He meant he was sorry, he meant he hated himself for the way he'd treated me. He had black moods because he had suffered, like Brick, and he couldn't always conquer them, but he loved me. He didn't want to hurt me—but sometimes he just couldn't help it.

"*I* like you," I said. "All the time."

136

"Then you're a fool," he said bitterly.

He doesn't believe *me,* I realized. He's never felt loved. He's as emotionally deprived as Brick. Thad's father had practically abandoned him, just as Brick's father had abandoned Brick. That's why he's this way. He can't conceive of anyone loving him the way he really is. That's probably why he became an actor and that's probably why he's acted the role of Brick for so long.

It was a revelation. All the puzzling pieces fit together perfectly, into a picture that explained everything. At last I could convince myself that he loved me.

He didn't pick me up the next morning. I thought maybe he was sick, but Amy told me at lunch that she'd just seen him in chemistry.

I waited outside Mr. Gelber's room for him. He didn't show up until the bell rang. He just nodded politely and went into the room.

He didn't wait for me when the class was over. He didn't drive me home. He didn't call me that night. When I phoned him Saturday evening, the maid said he was out.

I waited all Sunday for him to call me back, but he didn't.

On Monday I walked to school in a fog. I sat through my classes like a zombie. When seventh period was over I wanted to run out of school, to run home, because I was afraid to walk into Mr. Gelber's room.

But I didn't run. I forced myself to go to math, to

face whatever it was I'd have to face, because I knew I couldn't avoid it forever.

Thad wasn't outside the door, and I thought, just let him not be here, let me not have to see him, because I know he doesn't want to see me. I didn't understand why, or what had happened since Thursday, but as sure as I was then that he loved me, I was sure now that it was over.

I walked into the room and every head turned toward the door to watch me. Liza Mansfield was sitting on Thad's desk, making little circles on the back of his hand with one long, blood-red fingernail.

He heard the sudden hush. He looked up and saw me. For a second I saw guilt in his eyes, embarrassment. Then he quickly looked away and said something to Liza. She slid off his desk, but there was a very satisfied smile on her face.

I couldn't breathe. I was ready to turn and run, but the bell rang and Mr. Gelber came in right behind me and closed the door.

I moved toward my desk and it felt like I was trying to grope my way through wet curtains. This couldn't be real. This was a nightmare.

No matter what else he had done, or didn't do, or felt, for me—even if he didn't feel it now—I'd never thought Thad was capable of this. Not in front of a whole class, not when I had no place to run and no way to conceal my feelings.

Blindly I opened my math book.

When the bell rang I closed my book and reached down for my bag. I stood up. Thad was blocking my way. I was aware that people were watching us, that no one seemed to be racing out of the room, that it was unnaturally quiet.

"I'm sorry, Kate," he murmured. "I really am."

I looked into his eyes and let him see it all—everything I was feeling, every bit of pain he'd inflicted on me.

"Liar," I breathed. *"Liar."*

Sixteen

MY HEAD WAS pounding and my mouth tasted like acid. I could hardly see where I was going.

I thought I heard a car horn, but I didn't pay any attention to it.

"Katie. *Katie!*" Rob was standing right next to me on Fillmore Street, yelling in my ear.

I finally got him in focus. "Can I drive you home?" he asked. I nodded, and he helped me into the car.

I started to cry the moment he pulled away from the curb and once I started I couldn't stop. Rob didn't take me home, just drove on and on, I didn't know where, until I had a sodden lump of tissues in my hands, and when I looked out the window I saw boats and a dock.

He stopped the car. He looked at me, huddled against the door, a limp, ragged mess, and said, "I'm sorry, Katie."

"Why did he do it?" I asked. My voice was so hoarse I could hardly talk. "He said he loved me. Everything would have worked out. *He loved me last week.*"

"I'm sorry," he repeated. "I know how you feel."

"How could you?" I demanded. "How could you possibly understand how I feel?"

"You never cried like this over me," he said quietly.

For a moment I was too surprised to say anything. Then I said, "But you never did either. Over me."

"How do you know?"

I just sat there, stunned, uncomprehending, feeling as if I must be the stupidest person in the world.

"I'm sorry," I said finally. "I didn't realize—"

"I know you didn't," he said. "Maybe I'm not all that good at showing how I feel. But that doesn't mean I don't have any feelings."

"Rob, I don't know what to say. I just—"

"Don't. Please. Look, I know you need somebody right now, and I'm trying, but this is just . . . too hard. I can't be this close to you without wanting—I have to take you home now, Kate. Try and understand."

I didn't understand anything. Nothing. I had prided myself on my keen legal mind and I didn't know a thing about people, a thing about love.

I could do a complicated logic problem in two minutes, handle deductive and inductive reasoning, but, as Stephanie said, love wasn't logical. Love was emotions and chemistry and electricity, and laws that applied in labs didn't work the same way when you applied them to people.

Thad was right. You couldn't control what happened to you. You never could tell what would happen next even when you tried to write your own script. Fate—and all the other actors—kept ad-libbing.

How could I have been dumb enough to think that a fantasy could come true? I had been a fool—for believing in romance, for believing in fairy tales, for believing in happy endings.

I got through the rest of the week by holding my head high and ignoring the sympathetic gestures of my classmates, by never looking at Thad, by blinding myself to Liza Mansfield.

Amy and Stephanie would have come home with me every afternoon and stayed half the night, if I'd let them, but I didn't. I couldn't talk about it, not even to them. I didn't want to talk about it, or think about it.

The weekend was harder, because I couldn't blind myself to the images in my head, to what I pictured Thad and Liza were doing. I couldn't turn off my imagination. And I couldn't stop remembering every minute Thad had spent with me.

The next week was a little bit better; I just felt numb. When I didn't see Thad, when I managed to distract myself with studying, I could almost convince myself that I wasn't feeling anything at all.

The following Sunday he called.

"Katie, I have to talk to you."

I sat down heavily on a kitchen chair.

"I don't have anything to say to you."

"But there are things I have to say to you."

"Not one word that I'd believe." My voice was as cold as I could make it, as cold as I wanted to make my heart. "You're the biggest phoney of them all."

"You're right, but you don't know why. You don't understand how—"

"I don't want to understand."

"Katie, *please*. I'm going to wait at your corner. I can't come to your house. I can't face your parents. I'll

142

be there in ten minutes. I'm going to wait for you. I'll wait all night if I have to."

He hung up. It was five to six. I was cold all over. My stomach was churning. I went up to my room and started to play Wagner's Ring Cycle. I struggled not to feel anything, not to want anything. It was safer that way.

At six-thirty I looked out my parents' bedroom window. I could see the corner from there. The Jag was parked next to the stop sign.

I went back to my room.

At eight o'clock the car was still there. The street-light was on.

At ten of nine I went downstairs and told my parents I was going out for a while. I think what made up my mind was not that he'd waited there for three hours; it was what he'd said about not being able to face my mother and father.

"This late?" my mother said.

"I'm meeting someone."

"Oh. *Oh.*" They smiled, at me and then at each other.

I got my jacket and walked to the corner. Thad jumped out of the car and started to reach for me. I moved sideways to avoid him.

"I thought you wouldn't come," he said.

I shoved my hands in my pockets. "What do you want?"

"Katie, I've been so stupid."

"That makes two of us. Say what you have to say and let me go home."

"I can't say it like this, standing in the street. It's too

143

complicated. I have to make you understand." He put his hand on my arm.

"Don't you touch me!"

He backed off. "All right, I won't, I promise. Just, please, get in the car."

"Where are you taking me?"

"To my house. Just to talk. My mother's home, the maid's there, I don't blame you if you don't trust me, but I just want to talk to you, that's all. I'm not lying to you. I *never* lied to you."

This was so fantastic that I found myself getting into the car without any further protest. I told myself that I just wanted to hear whatever it was he had dreamed up to convince me that he'd never lied to me. It had to be stupendous—the biggest lie of all.

But when I settled into the front seat, and smelled the leather smell, I remembered the first time I'd been in that car, and the last time, and all the moments in between. They came back to me, all jumbled together, but as vivid as if they were happening right now. I'd deluded myself into thinking I could repress my feelings. I'd made a big mistake coming to meet him, and I never should have gotten into that car.

His house was bright when we parked in front of the garage. He came around to open the door for me, but didn't try and help me out of the car.

When we got inside, he led me to the library. All the lamps were lit. He closed the doors, and I remembered the last time he'd closed those doors and I felt like I was choking.

"Katie, sit down. Truth time," he said. "Okay?"

"That will make a nice change." I sat down on the couch.

"Listen," he began slowly. "I was lost here. From the day I walked into that school, I was lost. I didn't know how to act, I didn't know what normal people did. I've been working for almost ten years and all I learned was how to move in front of the camera, and not to believe anyone who says he'll call your agent in the morning. Before that I was in Washington and my father traveled all over and we went with him, like I told you, and I lived in embassies and hotels.

"But I wanted to try it—to just be ordinary for a while. All I knew about high school was what I saw on television. It looked like fun. I actually thought it would be a vacation for me, after working for so long, and never being with people my own age.

"But it was impossible. I realized that the first day. No one was going to treat me like any other kid. I don't know why I imagined they would."

"Did you rehearse this speech?" I asked coldly.

"Yes!" he cried. "For *days.*"

He started to pace around the room, restlessly, his hands in his pockets, his head down. Not like Brick now, not that prowling, caged walk—either he was as upset and confused as I was, or he was acting.

"And the things I had to catch up on to graduate. I was behind in everything. I noticed you the first day, in math. And when you came into Mr. Gelber's room and dropped your books—the minute I touched your hand, I felt it. And you did too, I could tell. And you know what happened then, Katie?"

"They didn't live happily ever after." There was no expression in my voice at all.

"No. Because you never loved me."

145

I jumped up from the couch in a rage. "How can you say that? Are you blind?"

"I wish I was. You were in love with a *character*. You were in love with a role I played."

"That's stupid!"

"Truth time," he insisted. "I was flattered that you had a crush on me because I liked you so much. I thought you'd get to know me, to see what I was really like, and it would be okay, but you didn't—you wouldn't. You never saw me—all you saw was a stupid, cardboard caricature dreamed up in Barbara Jo's head. And all you wanted from me was to be Brick Preston and sweep you off your feet."

"Oh, no," I said. I shook my head violently. I didn't want to listen to this. I didn't want to hear any more. "It's not true."

"It is true," he said. "And I didn't know what to do. All my life, whenever I found myself in a new situation, or whenever I was uncomfortable, I just put on an act and it usually worked out okay. Maybe you didn't realize it, but I didn't know what you expected from me. Until you told me."

I sank back down on the couch. He stood in front of me, just as he had the first time we were in that room. "You told me straight out what you wanted from me—what you wanted me to be. And you told me when you didn't even know you were telling me. The first time I kissed you you called me Brick. And I don't know how many times after that."

I could only sit there, watching him, watching his eyes.

"God, how I hate that stupid name. I hated it every time I heard you say it."

146

"But I thought that's what you were really like," I said desperately. "That's what you told me."

"No I didn't. That's what you wanted to believe. That's what you said you wanted. And I was so—attracted to you that I just—played the part."

"You were *acting?* The whole thing—it was an *act?*"

"From the night we went to the movies and you said I was real—Brick was real. That's when I gave up. Because I didn't think *you* ever would. I thought it would be easy. I mean, I've played the role for so long. But it got harder and harder . . . you don't know how hard it got."

"I don't believe it." I put my head down on the arm of the couch. "I don't believe it."

"I hated myself," he went on. "I hated the things I was doing, all the lines I had to say. But you liked it. It fit some crazy romantic fantasy you worked up, and I thought it would make you stay with me.

"But then I couldn't do it anymore. It wore me out, it made me sick—I couldn't stand hurting you."

"Why didn't you just *tell* me?"

"I should have. But I was afraid. I didn't know what to do. Not telling you was the lousiest thing of all."

"No," I said, "not quite."

"Ahh, Katie, it was so easy with her. She was so uncomplicated. She wanted to go out with an actor, she wanted to put another notch in her belt, she wanted me for my connections. A nice, straightforward opportunist. I could deal with that. I know people like her. You were hard, because I never knew anyone like you. Because I cared."

"So you staged a great, big, spectacular finale," I

said bitterly. "In front of a live audience. *Because you cared.*"

"No." He sat down next to me and leaned his elbows on his knees. He stared down at the rug. "Because I wasn't thinking. I was just trying not to hurt myself anymore. It wasn't deliberate. I didn't even think about her until she put a move on me. I never called her—she asked *me* out. I didn't realize it would attract that much attention. I mean, when I was with you, they really did seem to be accepting me, almost like anyone else. And when I wasn't with you anymore, I had no one. No friends."

I sat there letting all the things he'd said, all the things I hadn't wanted to hear, sink in. I replayed all our scenes together and remembered that even before I met him I had dreamed up a ridiculous fantasy of candlelit restaurants, a lifetime of bliss and black marble bathtubs. Complete with a musical score.

"But the party," I remembered. "You were so mean after the party. Everything was all right until then. What did I do?"

He stretched his legs out and leaned against the back of the couch with his hands behind his head. "You were so beautiful. I felt like I was torn in half. I wanted to be near you all the time, but I had to follow this crazy script I was acting. I thought you'd be nervous and shy—but you weren't. You didn't need me. You didn't seem like my nice, normal Katie anymore. I *was* jealous—and I thought I was going crazy. If I didn't act my part, you might not like me anymore, and if I did, I might lose you.

"I came late on purpose, you know. I sat by my door for forty-five minutes. I couldn't wait to see you, but that's what *he* would have done, so—"

"You were late on purpose?" I said incredulously. "You *wanted* me to be upset? You *wanted* me to be nervous and shy?"

"I *didn't* want it, don't you understand? It was part of the act. I'm not like that at all. I don't stand people up, I don't order people around, I don't—God, I never called anyone 'Baby' in my life. But you didn't know that. You didn't know anything about me. You never wanted to. When we got to your house after the party, when I kissed you, when I told you I loved you, you called me Brick. And when I treated you the worst, and felt the worst, you told me you still loved me—just the way I was. I couldn't go on with it."

"Take me home now," I whispered. "Please. I don't want to hear any more truth. I got the message. I made you hate yourself and you hate me for that. Okay. We're even."

"But Katie, I couldn't leave without—"

"You're leaving?" The sinking feeling in my stomach made me realize that I'd let myself hope, without admitting it, that after telling me all this, Thad would say, "Let's start over."

"Harry Kingman really *did* call my agent, believe it or not."

Think miniseries, I told myself crazily. Think prime time.

"But I thought you were sick of all that—you said everyone was a phoney—"

149

"Part of my script," he said. "I did exaggerate that a little. And I really did want to come to school here—but it didn't work out very well, did it?" He took a deep breath. "We're packing now. Leaving tomorrow."

"Your mother—the things you said about your mother—"

"I wouldn't make up something like that," he said reproachfully. "That was all true."

I got up and walked to the mahogany doors. My jacket was still on. I had never taken it off. I looked back at him, and he seemed so far away. Everything seemed so far away, like I was looking through the wrong end of binoculars.

And yet, maybe I was seeing more clearly than I had in weeks.

"Did it ever occur to you," I said, "that *you* might have had a preconceived idea about *me?* That you dreamed up a sit-com high school and a sweet little girl next door? And when *I* didn't fit *your* fantasy—"

He looked up sharply and started to say something. But he didn't. He just put his hand over his eyes for a moment as if the light bothered him.

I'd had enough. Too much. There was nothing left to say. I was drained of words, drained of energy.

"You can take me home now. I hope you feel better. I don't."

He pulled himself wearily off the couch. He looked exhausted. I had to concede that maybe I wasn't the only one who'd been hurt.

"I couldn't leave without explaining. I couldn't let you think—"

"But you *are* leaving! So what's the point?"

150

He picked up his jacket and walked toward me. He slid open the doors and stood there for a minute, looking into my eyes. When he spoke his voice was sad and quiet.

"Like you said, Kate. Maybe I have my own fantasies."

Seventeen

THAT WAS THE second week in March.

In April I got a postcard from Majorca. It read, "I am born again, by popular demand. Tune in next week for amazing details of my resurrection. I miss you. T.M."

I put the postcard carefully into my top dresser drawer. I took it out and reread it every day until the next one came.

It arrived the day they announced that Brick Preston hadn't been fatally wounded, despite the point-blank shots, the blood and the (sparsely attended) memorial service.

The postcard was from London. My mother, smiling broadly, handed it to me the moment I got home from school.

"Will be in NY next Fri—to stay—unless BP croaks again. Don't touch that dial—please see me in person. I dream about you. T."

"I take it you've read my mail," I said to my mother.

"It happened to be facing up when I took it out of the

box," she said shamelessly. "I just skimmed it, really. Will you see him?"

Will I?

Will Kate Bennett be able to forget about Brick Preston and forgive Thad Marshall?

Will Thad Marshall discover that Kate Bennett is the only woman he ever really loved?

Will he come back to New York and fly straight into Kate's open arms?

Will Kate's arms be open? Tune in next week. . . .

"Come on, Katie, this is your mother. You can tell me anything, remember? What are you going to do?"

I looked at the picture of Picadilly Circus on the postcard, but what I saw was his face and his eyes and the way he looked at me the night we went to the Japanese restaurant.

I started slowly up the stairs to put the postcard in my dresser drawer with the other postcard.

"Who knows how I'm going to feel next week?" I said dreamily. "You never can tell."

Well . . . almost never.

About the Author

Ellen Conford is an award-winning author of many books for young readers whose popularity stretches around the globe. Some of her books have been translated into Japanese, German, and Italian, and four have been made into TV specials.

Her previous Archway paperbacks include *Lenny Kandell, Smart Aleck* (a *School Library Journal* Best Book and winner of a *Parent's Choice* Award for Literature), *Hail, Hail Camp Timberwood* (winner of the 1983 California Young Reader Medal in the junior high category), and *To All My Fans with Love, from Sylvie* (winner of the IRA-CBC Children's Choice Award).

When she isn't writing, Ms. Conford enjoys doing crossword puzzles and watching old movies. She recently placed sixteenth in the U.S. Open Crossword Puzzle Championship. And, not surprisingly, she's become addicted to her VCR. Unlike Kate Bennett in YOU NEVER CAN TELL, she claims to "have a firm grip on reality and never spends more than an hour a day sitting near the phone waiting for Robert Redford to call."

Ms. Conford, a graduate of Hofstra University, lives in Great Neck, New York, and has "a husband, a kid, a cat, and a dog."